THE BRIEF INSANITY OF HERAKLES, THE WARRIOR

by

Walter Joseph Schenck, Jr.

Adapted from Euripides' play:

The Hercules Furens

416 B.C.E.

This work is dedicated to
my wife,
Molly Schenck,
my adventurous traveling partner.

We boldly walked the heartland of London,
crossing bridges, visiting castles,
Parliament, museums, taking trams, trains,
boats, journeys to parks, theaters, and Windsor.

And, of course,
Shakespeare's restored Globe Theatre.

Walter Joseph Schenck, Jr.,

Awards and Accolades

FAPA Award-winning author, Gold, 2014 –
Priests & Warriors
Category: Religion

FAPA Award-winning author, Silver, 2015 –
Shiloh, Unveiled
Category: Religion

FAPA Award-winning poet, Bronze, 2016 –
Thee & Me in a Mellow Thine
Category: Poetry

Royal Palm Literary Award, 1st Place, Gold, 2017 –
Catharine's Horses
Category: Biography

RECOMMENDED READ LIST
Kirkus Book Reviews:
First Voices

RECOMMENDED READ LIST
Kirkus Book Reviews:
Uncle Earl's Doggies

RECOMMENDED READ LIST
Kirkus Book Reviews:
Comprehensive Analysis of the Synoptic Gospels

Critical acclaim, Kirkus Book Reviews:
"Brilliantly existential book" –
The Birdcatcher

FEATURE AUTHOR in Publisher's Weekly:
The Birdcatcher

Royal Palm Literary Award, 2018 1st Place
Escape to Canada, Rendered in Poetic Overtures
Category: General Catch-All

Royal Palm Literary Award, 2018 1st Place
Hamlet, Reimagined
Category: Play

2018 Royal Palm Literary GRAND AWARD
The Dahris Clair Memorial Award for Play
Hamlet, Reimagined

Royal Palm Literary Award, 2018 3rd Place
A Glimpse of Peace on the Journey to Armageddon
Category: Novella

Royal Palm Semi-Finalist Award, 2018
Prometheus, Reimagined
Category: Science Fiction

Royal Palm Semi-Finalist Award, 2018
Prometheus, Reimagined
Category: Fantasy

FAPA Silver Award-winner, 2019
How to Correctly Format A Stage Play
Category: Research

Royal Palm Literary Award, 2019 1st Place
Blemished, The Stage Play
Category: Play

Royal Palm Literary Award, 2019 2nd Place
Tribulations of Yonah, The Prophet
Category: Novella

Nominated for 2018 Florida Humanitarian Award –
Literature

Professional membership in PEN American Central

Professional membership in Dramatists Guild

Concerning the Stage Play Formatting

As I am a Professional member of the Dramatists Guild of America, I asked the organization quite a few questions concerning the proper formatting of a stage play, especially in consideration of their two format offerings in Final Draft. After several ideas were explored, I decided to create a universal format applicable to all stage plays and entitled it *How to Correctly Format A Stage Play.*

The formatting in this version will seem strange at first glance, but it is mathematically precise, obeying the strict parameters set out in the published guideline. This formula meets the approval of the Dramatist Guide.

Briefly:

1. Fonts must always be Courier New 12 point font while the page should be 8.5 inches by 11 inches, or, letter size.

2. Dialogue begins at 1.5 inches from the left edge without indentation.

   a. Right hand side of the dialogue will be jagged, unless the author intentionally justifies the text. The jagged formatting is to honor the historic usage of manual typewriter. If the author justifies the dialogue, and there are over two paragraphs, each paragraph should be indented .25 inch.

3. Character names are to be centered in caps with .5 inch offset (to emphasize the preceding action on the second line), and centered.

   a. A character's name should never end the page, but rather, should be placed on the top of the following page.
   b. The character's moods, actions, and directions should be enclosed inside parentheses centered directly underneath the character's name.

CHARACTER'S NAME CAPS with .05 inch offset
(Parentheses action line is centered.)

4. CAST OF CHARACTERS offset by 4.5 inches from left
   edge of the paper with jagged text on right-hand
   side. Can be either justified or not.

5. Exit and enter directions on the extreme right side
   with character names in caps, enclosed in
   parentheses, 5.5 inches from the left margin.

                                        (Exit THOMAS)

                                        (Enter WIFE)

6. Stage Directions and Dialogue instructions are
   properly placed 3 inches from left margin with a
   maximum range of 6.5 inches, rendered within
   parentheses, justified only if the dialogue is
   jagged left.

1.

                    (For example: stage directions are
                    justified block only when the
                    dialogue is jagged left.)

                            MOLLY
Hello Walter. This is Molly, your wife's friend. How are
things going for you today? I heard you're taking a vacation
to Costa Rica. Can you bring me back a shawl and a few other
things?

2.

                    (Stage directions and instructions
                    are jagged left when the dialogue
                    is justified.)

                                MOLLY
   Hello Walter. This is Molly, your wife's friend. How are
things going for you today? I heard you're taking a
vacation to Costa Rica. Can you bring me back a shawl and a
few other things?

   7. Character orphans. Do not end the page with a
       character's name. Create a new page with the name
       centered and offset by .5 inches on the top of the
       next page.

   8. ACTs and Scenes are placed 5 inches from the left
       margin. ACTS is in caps while Scenes is rendered in
       caps and lowercase.

   9. SETTING begins at left margin with location offset
       at 4.5 inches.

   10. Dialogue interruption occurs when a person enters
       or exits during the speech. When the original
       speaker continues his dialogue, place the same
       character's name in the center of the page with the
       [CON'T] designation after the comma.

   While a screenplay utilizes (), a stage play uses [].

                               THOMAS
Goodbye.

                                          (Exit WIFE)

                                          (Enter SON)

                          THOMAS, [CON'T]
How are you?

                          Special Note:
Please do not confuse the dialogue interruption of the

stage play with the action line of a screenplay.

I also discussed with the Dramatist Guild the usage of
MORE whenever the dialogue shifts from one page to the
next and they assured the placement of MORE is only
used by the screenplay format. The usage of
"Continued" is not incorporated in either format of
FINAL DRAFT.

Concerning the Dialogue Stresses

As I am working with a Greek play written nearly twenty-five centuries ago, I had to become acutely aware of the existing English translations and their emphasis on how they recreated their versions and in what manner they rendered the English sentence with their peculiar stress. On first reading I could readily understand the translators' anxieties concerning their translations. To approach my task, I assigned myself reading material from 1809 through 1954. At first, I wanted to render my version in modern 21st century English, but the nuances of 21st century English lost their flavors. I rethought my approach and dismissed it, thinking a paraphrased version would become a shameful disregard of the original Greek translators' hard work. Understanding this, I carefully studied how the dialogue was translated into English, necessitating an extensive review of Rev. Robert Potter, Arthur Way, Theodore Buckley, Gilbert Murray, and a few others' work. When I came to understand the harmonics and rhymes of Greek tragedies, absorbing the style of "Unrhymed Alexandrine," I felt ready to proceed on my own.

The Greek dialogue relies on a formal meter consisting of six stresses, which makes it an awkward English reading experience. The translators, limited by the nuances of the original Greek dialogue, rendered their English translations into a near agony, transposing words into a different reading experience. The thing is, after reading a lot of variant renderings, I began to think like the 18th and 19th century translators. Suddenly, modern English became boring and unskilled. Modern English seemed colorless, lacking harmonic dynamics. I even began speaking as if I lived in the 19th century, which of course made me seem quite odd to the listener who must have wondered what spaceship I just stepped out of.

Thus, it seemed appropriate for me to create this play in as modern an English as possible, while still adhering to the ancient Greek playwrights' usage of stresses in their sentences. It also seemed appropriate for me to render the dialogue as I did due to my incorporation of Greek gods and Achaeans intermixing with one another.

I also wanted to write this play in an elevated English as street English seemed disharmonious to the task.

Therefore, the reality the reader must face is that dialogue spoken by the Greeks is different from popular English. As the Greeks lived in a different era with their own cultural values and expressive harmonics and nuances, I felt it my responsibility to stay within their scope.

Also, because this play relies on Greek mythologies, the play is populated with several tough to pronounce Greek names. This is another reality of touching upon Greek performances.

To create an original play, based on an existing play known throughout the world, required quite an arduous undertaking. Every single word has been changed while trying to make it feel as though nothing changed. To take on Euripides, while maintaining his flavor, challenged me to quite an exhausting degree. The research was incredulously difficult. I hope, when the play readers approach my material, they do so with a kind heart.

AUTHOR'S SUGGESTION TO THE DIRECTOR

Though this is not a musical, nor requires a musical score, if at all possible, something akin to Stravinsky's music can be played during the twelve reenactments of ACT 2, Scene 2, the dancing rendered as a ballet.

CONTENTS

Concerning the
    Stage Play Formatting

Cast of Characters

ARGUMENT

DRAMATIS PERSONAE

Amphitryon: Husband of Alkmena. He adopts
                                     Herakles after Zeus abandoned
                                     his bastard child.

Megara: Wife of Herakles.

Lykus: A usurper, king of Thebes.

Herakles: Zeus is his true father after
                                     having an illicit affair with
                                     Herakles' mother, Alkmena.

Theseus: Herakles cousin. Fights
                                     alongside him in Tartarus.

Iris: Hera's companion. A Goddess.

Lyssa: Owner of Cerberus.

Theseus: King of Athens.

Leader of the Theban Elders: The Chorus.

Servant of Herakles

ADDIONAL CHARACTERS

Therimachus, Deicoon,
and Creontiades: The three young sons of
                                     Herakles.

Attendants of Lykus and of Theseus

CHARACTERS BY REFERENCE

Kreon: Herakles best friend. Former
                                     king of Thebes. Assassinated
                                     by Lykus.

Eurystheus: Herakles' stepbrother and
                                     master.

ARGUMENT

Herakles was hated, from his birth, by Hera. Through her manipulative cunning, she enslaved his advanced and intuitive warrior skills to Eurystheus, king of Argos.

After eleven great struggles and near-defeats, Herakles was tasked again to wage a twelfth great battle against the Hound of Tartarus: Cerberus, capturing it alive as evidence of his superior fighting skills.

Before he journeyed on his designated quest to battle the ferocious, three-headed monster conjoined to three-bodies, its birth from the womb of Echidna through the impregnation of her lover, Typhon: the deadly serpentine giant, Herakles determined first to protect his family against retribution by an enraged master should he fail in his mission.

After embracing his adoptive father, Amphitryon, after affectionately kissing Megara, his wife, he and Theseus, his cousin, escorted them to their trusted friend, King Kreon of Thebes.

For nine worrisome months, after he descended into the Land of Darkness, no one heard from Herakles or Theseus. The long absence encouraged Lykus, an ambitious man from Euboea, to persuade the corrupt merchants and political leaders to appoint him as their new ruler, resulting in Kreon's assassination.

Afraid for their safety, many of Herakles' friends sought sanctuary in the Temple of Zeus, offering lamentations and animal sacrifices, fervently praying for a savior to avenge them of King Kreon's murder.

Hera, hearing, determined to murder Herakles, he who as a baby bit off her nipple, her spilled milk, forming the nucleus of the Milky Way.

ACT 1

Scene 1

SETTING: Inside the deep caverns of
                                Tartarus, frightful pleads of
                                agony encompass the stage. A
                                monstrous, gigantic image of
                                CERBERUS appears: its foul
                                distorted mouths salivating as
                                its three heads snap
                                ferociously. In place of a
                                tail, the conjoined dog's
                                three bodies show the long head
                                of a poisonous snake,
                                vigorously moving.

                                The stage light shines over the
                                body of fully naked THESEUS
                                chained to the left side.
                                Flames from the floor shoot up
                                in front of him, followed by
                                his screams.

AT RISE: Fully naked HERAKLES, armed
                                with a large shield and sword
                                heroically swings onto the
                                stage from above, landing
                                directly in front of THESEUS,
                                facing the monstrosity. He
                                stands in full frontal strive,
                                allowing the audience to fully
                                view his naked body as he
                                powerfully strikes at
                                CERBERUS.

                        HERAKLES
     Depraved offspring from Echidna and Typhon, I command
you, stay and obey.

                                (Enter HERA, LYSSA,
                                IRIS, all scantily
                                dressed in
                                translucent
                                clothes.)

                         HERA
          It is you who must stay, eternally.

                         IRIS
          . . . and obey the ax's eternal cry against the hardened
          granite walls. Surrender your sword.

                         LYSSA
          Let him keep his sword. Cerberus, kill him.

                              (Flames emit again from the floor as
                              a slight mist surrounds the actors.
                              HERAKLES shouts fiercely as he
                              rushes forward to the three
                              goddesses, capturing LYSSA, holding
                              his sword underneath her throat.)

                         HERAKLES
          It is you who will surrender. Otherwise, perish.

                         HERA
          She is an empowered goddess of the Council Chambers of
          Olympus. You cannot kill an empowered goddess.

                         HERAKLES
          Just as I could not bite off your breast's nipple, yet I
          did, didn't I, forever disfiguring you as a mockery among
          all the goddesses. Lyssa's head, her blind eyes, her
          gapping mouth holding a swollen, unspeaking tongue, her
          pointed ears, her purple hair will look fantastic, don't
          you agree, inside my trophy case? As for you Iris, you're
          not worth more than a common flower: wilting shamefully in
          a vast array of white and pink lilies.

                         HERA
          Arrogant! Despicable! Savage bastard! Release Lyssa.
          Athena is not here to protect you from my avenging wrath.

                              (The dog's three heads growl
                              harshly.)

                         HERAKLES
          Eurystheus commanded me to tame this beast. Yet, I
          believe I prefer to kill the mutt and tame this bitch.

                              (LYSSA screeches.)

LYSSA
You damn fool. Let go of me. I am the goddess of raging insanity in the minds of men and the afflicter of rabies in all animals. I am the daughter of Nyx, sister of Thanatos, the last child of castrated Uranus birthed from the gushing pool of his agonized blood spillage.

IRIS
Thanatos: save your sister!

                              (Enter THANATOS.)

THANATOS
Mighty Herakles in my realm. IN MY REALM! O how cunningly you evaded Charon, the boatman of the river Styx, not so much as the smallest coin paid. But Thebes, he's that coin of entry, isn't he?
                    (THANATOS points his arm directly to
                    THESEUS, sending his body into
                    spasmodic fits of pain.)
Release my sister.

HERAKLES
Do you think I will so willingly release her? I, who journeyed across the treacherous slopes of the darkened Jaws of Taenarus to reach this destiny's declaration of mortal man conquering grave evil? On what terms?

THANATOS
Terms? What can a mortal offer me?

HERAKLES
I am a wrestler, famed throughout Greece. Undefeated. I heard, through Athena, you are also a famed wrestler, undefeated. Your sister's life a trade for an obedient dog and for Theseus' and my life should I defeat you.

THANATOS
A death match?

HERAKLES
A death match!

THANATHOS
And what coinage shall you pay Charon for Theseus and your entry?

                              HERAKLES
My shield for Theseus. My sword for myself.

                              THANATOS
The wager is sealed.

                    (Thunderous sounds erupt throughout
                    the stage as both figures clasp each
                    other's arms, wrestling furiously.
                    The dog furiously growls and snaps
                    at HERAKLES whenever THANATOS pushes
                    the dog near him. HERA suddenly trips
                    HERAKLES, and falling, he grabs
                    THANATOS' shoulders, pulling him
                    over his head, clutching his
                    shoulders as he pins THANATOS' back
                    to the floor, afterward clutching
                    his throat tightly until he nearly
                    faints. THANATOS' slaps HERAKLES'
                    shoulder, surrendering.)

                              HERAKLES
Victory is mine.

                    (HERAKLES rolls away from THANATOS,
                    instantly grabbing his sword,
                    pointing the edge directly at HERA'S
                    waist.)

                              THANATOS
Victory is yours. Lyssa, remove your spell from Cerberus.
Permit the tamed and obedient dog to follow Herakles
wherever he goes. Theseus. You are free.

                              HERA
Herakles. Kill me now. This is not the end of my plagues
against you.

                              LYSSA
Before you leave Hades, I swear I will destroy you! You,
your wife, your sons, and all your friends.

(Exit ALL.)

(LIGHTS FADE.)

(CURTAINS.)

(END OF SCENE 1.)

ACT 2

Scene 1

SETTING: At Thebes, before the Temple
                                of Zeus.

AT RISE: AMPHITRYON, MEGARA, and her
                                three sons by HERAKLES, sit
                                on the steps of the altar of
                                Zeus the Deliverer.

AMPHITRYON

   Rumors and gossip afflict my life. Whispers of the true
parentage of Herakles abound in unlimited fashion, without
discretion: Amphitryon or Zeus, the god of gods. Zeus the
charmer, the seducer of ten-thousand women, the birther of
five-thousand sons, vanquishing a woman's resistance before
a second heartbeat can sound or a second breath emitted.
Zeus, the perfecter of bestiality in the guise of bull,
lion, goat, goose, fathering children of ill-repute: the
corrupt demeaners of hybrid men imposing unlawful laws
against all mortal men born true from the original man,
created in the image of Prometheus, shaper and impregnator
of clay.
   My wife, Alkmena, of royal blood, descended from Perseus,
the monster slayer, founder of Mycenae, destroyer of the
Gorgon, Medusa. Perseus, savior of Andromeda, his wife,
from Cetus the terror whale of Ethiopia. Alkmena,
acknowledged as the legal mother of Herakles as recorded by
the Keeper of Historic Records. This, my wife, I love, and
in love forgive her betrayal when Zeus the seducer placed
upon himself my shape, form, and face, beguiling her to
surrender her bed for lust filled treachery.
   Years later, my anger aroused, father and son, enjoined
on a quest of salvation, finding none. Then, enjoined on a
life anew, still, we failed to embrace the gift of
salvation, remaining mortals, jesters for the gods' glee.
   Disappointed, we nevertheless journeyed onward to an
expectation of renewal, driven firstly by an erroneous
murder of Electryon. With unthinking impulsiveness, I
slammed my club in anger, striking dead Electryon. Beside
myself for having murdered the father of my bride, Alkmena,
I ran away to Thebes to escape my persecutors. I often
think of that angry moment, wondering if it was
self0driven, or motivated by fate designed. Never before

had I thought of living in Thebes, but by destiny's design, my hasty flee settled me in the City of Thebes. Here, love blossomed in the shape of beautiful Megara in my son's eyes. Megara, daughter of warriors' breed, trained conquerors and defenders: the dragon race of courage, unafraid . . . the Kadmus. In their city we settled. Yes, among them we discovered refuge, our fears temporarily dispelled.

From the seed of these forward-thinking citizens sprang Kreon, son of Menoekeus, king . . . my son's best friend, protector immaculate.

Then when the drums and echoing shouts for war against Minyae roared, Herakles and I marched, armed, among the soldiers sworn to protect Thebes. Victorious, generous in gifts, Herakles was given the rank of General, while I, became his counselor, indivisible. The greatest award, Herakles' pledged marriage to Kreon's daughter, Megara.

Where sounds today the wondrous marriage flutes of happiness after my son, Herakles, abandoned her and his delightful children for his twelfth anointed task?

Whatever, whenever, Eurystheus demands, enslaved servant, Herakles, obeys. Now, inside Argive walls and Cyclopean streets exists I, yet, for how long?

In the city of Thebes, I am a criminal condemned. The children of fallen Elektryon have discovered me and upon that discovery, offered rewards, assuring me a ghostly departure. Virtuous Megara, innocent Therimachus, Deicoon, and Creontiades, children born in graceful tranquility, adored by Herakles, now wait in somber fear for death's visitation.

Through cunning and disguise, I will find a way to avert death's timeframe, adding hours, weeks, months, and possibly even years, to my lifespan. This hope I shall endeavor to make real.

Hera, hateful Hera, and truthfully, should it not be I who hates her for not directing, for not plotting, her brother/husband's death? Why should she focus her ornate skills and cunning toward murdering my son: an innocent born in strength, suffering forever a rage unwarranted. Herakles, however, listens to Athena's wisdom . . . and, in turn, my son's sins, published in the Keeper's manifest, are discarded.

All, except one.

What value has Herakles' past achievements brought to him when a new trial arises? Lust for glory is not his, but belongs solely to Eurystheus who boasts of warriors', untamed, who reside among his palace's rooms, living solely to perform the desires and wages that the Grecian cities announce, broadcasting grand feats for the poets' prosperity.

Though vice deplored is revealed through treachery, enlightened, vice's secrets become nothing more than a tainted rumor. Under such circumstances, came forth my son, mighty in virtue and deeds performed, set upon a journey of death, murdering, if need be, those who oppose his task. Theseus, his cousin, determined to travel with him, as a quest, pondered and established in the gambling tables of odds innumerable-the token of whim, the manifest value of rulership.

On a morning pained and sad, tears shed with memorable sharing, departed two souls transfixed on an energized mission to conquer the brilliant scheme of fallen boulders haphazardly obstructing the path's downward slope into the gorge of Tainarus—the promise of corpses, a vulture's delight—the theft of courage an expected betrayal, thus thought the chronicler as the months expired, silence deafening the streets of Thebes: the forceful, brightening flames from the seven towers, unanswered.

Upon this silence, upon this heightening tiers of Cadmean fire and smoke, appeared Lykus, an Euboean by birth, a Theban by conquest, claimer to the throne through an inheritance pledged by Zethus and Amphion, twin children of Zeus through intercourse with Antiope, daughter of the Boeotian river god Asopus.

Upon the lowering slopes of Cithaeron appeared Lykus from the heavy mists hovering the banks of mystical plight, accompanied with armed mercenaries. With brazen skills and diplomatic maneuverings, he galloped ahead of his forces in a chariot pulled through tumultuous streams and caking mud. With deceit filled ambition, anxiety his manifest written in the stars, the Keeper of Historic Records wrote down in tearful alphabet the exact moment of King Kreon's decapitation, Lyssa's glory sweetly sung in harmonic balance with Lyssa's melodic rhythm.

In this horror of horrors descended upon us as a fear enshrouded, this cancerous mandate to murder virtuous Megara and her three innocent children: Therimachus, Deicoon, and Creontiades. Trusting, they placed their teary eyes upon me, beseeching me for their salvation from the unknown terrors afflicting their existence. I, upon a blood-stained cloth, fell on my knees, opening my arms to receive first the harsh blow of frightful death on the epicenter of the altar of Zeus.

When Lykus' arms lifted his sword, readying it to strike fiercely, a bathing beam of radiating light encompassed the alter of Zeus, displacing the gigantic mass of shadowing clouds. From within the clouds issued forth an ethereal voice, an uncanny experience, removing from the minds of ambitious slayers . . . hateful terror. In a smoothness never felt beforehand, a ceasing of violence ensued, the Savior Zeus in fond memory recalling in each hearer's mind Herakles saving his Temple from destruction by the willful rage of the Minyae conquerors. This voice of tranquility turned the desperately stressed desire of committing murder to a state of quiet reflection akin to calm.

(Enter ZEUS.)

ZEUS

Lykus, do not kill Herakles' children, nor Megara, his wife, nor Amphitryon, his adoptive father. Herakles has undertaken an enormous task, fearlessly engaging perils never before faced by warrior or slayer: the taming of Cerberus.

All those, who seek sanctuary at my altar, are granted sanctuary. Though the doors of Theban houses have been shuttered by your fallacious cowards, all who are here will be provided food, water, fruits, vegetables, and protection from the rains. Do not harm any of them. This is my gift to the hero who saved my altar from desecration by the hordes of Minyae.

(Exit ZEUS.)

AMPHITRYON

May those, who had been our friends, remain our friends. Allow them, without interference, to provide for us the essentials to keep us alive. If they prefer not to help us, so let it be as they wish. A true friend will never betray a true friend. If they are unable to help us, though they try, let them remain our friends. If, through evil's selection, they refuse to assist us, evil's manifestation cannot be thwart, for it beckons to enrich the poor and promote the rich to power. The stern reality of survival faces all of us. How we cope within its vice determines our worth . . . or our folly.

MEGARA

Great and Wise Counselor, you are old. You can no longer advise generals and kings how to lead armies, much less raise up your own sword. Cherish in your final moments, memories of your once grand power when you led the vast Theban army with their upturned spears across hallowed ground to vanquish victoriously all her enemies. Permit the gods their humor. Their jests fill the empty space with reflective scenes of glories performed by mortal men. Let them believe they mold our outcomes, when in fact, it is so easy for all of us to forget who they are, replacing their names with other names, their continued existence dependent on the culture of current might.

Wealthy, powerful Kreon. Gold-hammered chairs, gold encrusted tables, gold-worked statues, golden cups of wine poured from golden molded jars, where is he now? Headless. A corpse whose once thriving arms and legs lie rigid and rotting atop a dung-heap of bloodied rags, waiting for the torches' glow to enflame his carcass into a small mound of ashes, dispersed by the wind to wherever it chooses, without a single protest.

Kreon once had sons, just as I now have sons. My brothers perished moments after his head slammed and tumbled upon the ground. Kreon, my father, dead, dying uselessly for naught, his anticipated inheritance to his sons, stolen by an artful thief. He who was great, in less than a year, will be forgotten. Not even his symbolic long lance of rulership will survive the coming fire.

O, ancient man, do not desire renown or a single extra moment of life. It will be your undoing. You and I have become targets for the arrows. Remember now precious memories. I cling upon this moment reflections of my embraces within Herakles' arms and his gift to me to bring into this world the wondrous lives of our children. As an enraged woman, filled with the burst of righteous energy, I will rise up and shelter my children with my own body, the arrows piercing first me, then alas, perhaps through mercy, one of my three, may live.

                    THERIMACHUS
  Mother, where is our father?

                      MEGARA
  He has journeyed to the Caverns of Mists and Mysteries.

                      DEICOON
  Why there?

MEGARA

In idle jest the jokester gods of Olympus convinced him to bring from there to his master, a tame dog.

CREONTIADES

When will father return to us with the dog?

MEGARA

The dog is a gift to his master. It is not for us to pet. Together, let us pray to Zeus for your father's quick return.
(To AMPHITRYON.)
See, father, how their innocent minds work? Like me, like all Thebans loyal, they want Herakles to return to us. They to hug. Me to rekindle our affection. The Thebans to rally around a conquering hero. For endless hours, each time the door opened, the children eagerly rushed to it expecting to meet their father. Instead, they only found the breadman, or the cheese maker, with their hands open for payment. They dream of galloping upon their father's knees and riding upon his back as though he were a protecting horse, safely crossing the brook toward unencountered adventures.

Father, while we have sat here, waiting for satisfying nourishment and quenching water, have you devised any plans to escape from here? I do not know the landscape's contours as well as you do. I do not know what streets to cross, in which corners to hide, what safe houses to run toward. It appears all seven gates are well guarded. The torch lights are too bright. Have we any friends we can trust? Please, share with me something comforting, otherwise, I will die from the anxiety afflicting my heart.

AMPHITRYON

Daughter, we have no friends on any safe streets. We must remain patient and pray for Herakles return.

MEGARA
(Laughing.)
Herakles to the rescue. How often have I heard that one? It seems you deliberately intend to hasten me toward my death. Do you love yourself so much you will sacrifice me to keep yourself alive?

AMPHITRYON

Yes, I'm happy to be alive . . . not dead as the frozen corpses still lingering on the streets of destruction. However, I will die for you. For the children. I will not retreat nor utter unkind words against you. You are my son's wife, therefore, my daughter. Rejoice with me that we have a champion to look towards. Life is not only love, life is hope.

                           MEGARA
   Today, anguished hopelessness and dread encompass my life. Yesterday was nothing more than a lotus potion enrapturing my hours with hazy fantasies.

                          AMPHITRYON
   Every moment we remain alive, is victory against evil.

                           MEGARA
   The suspense of life, does it not nag at you with the deepest onslaught of anguish? These are not kind moments to either one of us, despite any smile you can muster.

                          AMPHITRYON
   Daughter, violent winds calm.
   Ferocious storms abate.
   Raging sea storms, at times, can carry crew and captain to a destination only dreamed of.
   My son, your husband, will rescue us.
   Think of the happy moments you two spent together, thus alleviating the flow of tears upon your smooth cheeks.
   The tempest furies recede.
   Legends exist to soothe our souls.
   The corrupt politicians will eventually die as will all the fakers and liars.
   Herakles shall always remain our hero.
   With unmitigated trust, let us sleep, so when we wake, it will be with the new dawn of freedom.
   Stop despairing.
   You are not a coward.

                              (Enter the CHORUS,
                              led by the LEADER
                              OF THE THEBAN
                              ELDERS.)

                              (The old men rely on their staves to
                              support and balance their movements
                              as they struggle up the steep
                              incline of Zeus' altar.)

LEADER OF THE THEBAN ELDERS

   With spirit and might: with firm hearts resolute, determined, we will climb upward to the very tops of the temple roof.
   Climb upward, without hesitation. Rest only when foot and hand alight upon the very top. Only then, with elbow and knee perched, with glorified eyes viewing the vastness our lands, only then will we set our thoughts on planning a way to free us to enjoy and embrace once again the wonders of our gracious homeland.

   Let your staff bend and your shoulders bow.
   Let your ankles ache and your thighs tighten.
   Add to your voice genuine sorrow, for our chants
   Of dire defeat are a homage to Zeus.

   Raise your voice to the clouds, so the trumpeter swan can bellow our anguished torments to the ears of Zeus.
   Let the Red-crested Pochard carry forth our message before Lykus' mercenaries silence us, rendering our breathes into a ghostly phantom.
   The night's plead is nothing more than a nightmare's scream . . . our future is numbed by paralysis.
   Remembrances of yesterday's glory a dismal heartache.

   Who shall then plead to Zeus to remember our friends long since dead, their fatherless children meandering through the streets in undignified disrespect: the treasured names and reputations of great families scorned.
   No one is left to mourn for the master of the house, the once dignified king's mansion nothing more now than a whore's dwelling.

   Brothers! Climb onward and conquer the steep incline.
   Refuse for your tired feet and exhausted body to rest.
   Your aching and sore arms must continue to grope upward.
   Pulverize the stones beneath your body into a soft layer of sand and transform aching muscles into the youthful vigor of a young warrior.
   Set free your spirits so your body may float over creviced and split boulders.

   Look no further than to the Grecian horse—a warrior's companion, a farmer's friend, the merchant's benefactor—the puller of weights and burdens through treacherous trails and unexplored plains, two teams combined one behind the

other, as a team they task themselves toward the completion
of their assigned tasks.

    Stretch forth your strong hand to the weaker hand.
    Extend the helm of your garment for another to grasp.
    Should one fall, help him up.
    If a tree branch blinds his path, cut it away so another
may cross the same path unburdened.

    Do not be ashamed to ask for help.
    On this steep incline of salvation, we are equal to one
another, old swords and young shields desire the same
venue.
    The toils of our battle-spears are sharpened for one
purpose only: so that when we stand united, shoulder-to-
shoulder, our lines resolved to stand, when the spears
clash, for the honor of country and family: advance.

    We are the fathers and breeders of intense-defying
dragons.
    The eyes of youth glare with hostility at our enemies.
    Our children, not us, are the protectors and enhancers of
our ideologies. O, may the corruptors not twist our hard-
won themes into a trifled dismissive.
    Should it happen that our children are slaughtered in
totality, what recourse for us: their parents, but to
follow them in death, not in dirge loud, but in silent
repentance for having failed to teach them the necessity of
endurance regardless of the harmful and overwhelming charge
against them.

    Let our children on the battlefield first see our eyes
before they see the eyes of the enemy, so in offensive
posture they will press hard to victory their parents'
values. Though slain, behold the dead in somber pride-O
what a majestic troop they are: the champions of our land.

    For now, however, hush. Lykus and his armed mercenaries
advance rapidly toward us.

                              (Enter LYKUS.)

                    LYKUS
    Amphitryon, I accept that you are indeed the Father of
Herakles. As to your daughter-in-law, I question the
validity of Kreon's legitimate right to marry her to a man
who is always wandering about the world killing animals and

harming men. He is a novel of hostilities married to a woman of graceful manners. Why would Kreon permit such a union?

More than that, I wonder, why in the world either of you would desire to prolong your life for a second more, knowing the harshness of the man you both claim as a profound effect over your beings. What effect? The dismal reputation of a drunkard? An adulterer? A murderer? An advantage manipulator of plight-filled lives who are correctly assigned the energies to survive?

Why would you want a degenerate has-been to attempt your rescue when you are already tarnished with a filthy associate? There is no value of being the father, or the wife, of such a scorned filled man of such disgustingly low repute.

He will not save you from imminent disaster.
                    (Pauses to stare at the three
                    sons.)

                         MEGARA
My husband and the father of my children lives and strives in glorious conquest for he is more than a man . . . he is a demigod.

                         LYKUS
Why do you believe that the contemptuous breeder of these three degenerates still lives? Surely you know he perished in the confines of Hades. How stupid you are to cling to a false hope he still breathes-for the breaths he takes are the thefts of breaths from everyone better deserving than he the oxygen in his lungs.

One morning soon you will wake to down-pointed spears, And through the merest smile on my lips, die.

                         MEGARA
Die I shall and descend to Pluto's room when he beckons me forth. Living Herakles will avenge me.

                         LYKUS
The fool never carried a shield. Never threw a spear. Never sharpened a sword. No. He brags through every tavern of his exploits, but when you look at him, what do you see? A naked man with a flaccid penis, armed with only an aged bow and the leftover limbs forming his impossible to shoot-straight arrows. Herakles is a jokester's coward. Only the ugliest and oldest whores have sex with him.

How is that you, a barely average looking woman, with smallish breasts and thicken waist, could believe your irresponsible husband is a warrior born from the semen of Zeus?

MEGARA

A man, confident in his strength, need not be armed with spear, shield, and sword. He, alone, killed the hydra of the marshes and with his hands strangled to death the Nemean lion. Such deeds resided deep in the memory of the people, and for his courage, the people love his three sons and have pledged to protect his family, even though Kreon, my father, was murdered by you. And, how did you overpower my brother. Jocasta? Through a face-to-face battle? Or, in the darkened hallways of confusion where ten mercenaries beat him to death before you dared to show your face to me.

LYKUS

Is this how you plan to survive your ordeal? Through delusional delusions? When you close your eyes this night, think how impossible it is for a crooked arrow to be shot straight, especially by a coward to afraid to come near his target. Shall I, for your children's sake, arm your husband with a spear so he can lounge it at me? Say yes, and I will. Afterward, I will laugh when he flings the spear at me, missing me by a far margin. His eyes will sweat with the sweat of a faker discovered in the absolute worst moment of an imposter's dream: the moment of quaranteed death.

(To AMPHITRYON.)

Without regret, without hesitation or the slightest pause, I plunged my sword through Kreon's neck, freeing a stupid man's irrational thinking brain from his rationally strong body. Now the vultures have consumed his eyes, nose, flesh, and ears while the feral dogs feasted on his body. I stand guilty before you. I boast about my victory over him. I pride myself on my treachery. Now, I laugh at you who stand here afraid, dreading me for a deed well accomplished. Today, I am the true king of Thebes. And, here, though this is the Temple of Zeus, are the three sons of Herakles whose best friend I killed with the upmost pleasure.

Did you know, Amphitryon, that I can see the future. Yes. I see these three boys growing up, and having loved their uncle, Kreon, will wage war against me, upon a future battlefield, leading soldiers in a tight formation. These upstarts will face my mercenaries when they grow up. They

will become the generals of avenging Thebans, waging war to
decapitate my own head.

   This foreseen event, I will now avert by slowly removing
their own heads from their shoulders before they grow up to
remove my own head from my shoulders. I am going to relish
every scream they scream.

                         AMPHITRYON

   Plots and deceits shall disgorge your conceit.
In vain necessity you liken my son to a human's fallacious
weakness: a drunkard and a coward his label for your
pleasure. Yet, what if I am not Herakles' father bred true?
What instead if it is Zeus who is Herakles' father bred
true? If thus correct, who shall defend Herakles? Myself?
Or, Zeus. If I, kill Herakles' children. I cannot defend
them. If Zeus, dare not harm them for what mortal can
defend or justify to Zeus, Charon's refusal to cross the
Styx? Do you dare to take a chance for your eternal soul to
drift aimlessly in a quagmire of harmful vices, with
screams so horrific who will stop to listen to the root
cause of your agony?

   What man, god, demon, or saint will take pity on a child-
murderer, who though having mistaken the genuine identity
of his jealous target, will permit him to seek refuge
within their darkest harbor, so isolated, only scurrying
monsters can dwell within its cantankerous dimension? It is
best to believe Herakles is not mortal. It is best to
believe Herakles, alone, can listen to Zeus' thunderous
call without fear as he sets forward on his death-defying
tasks to conquer abstractions to horrific to imagine. No.
Go on. Think Herakles a coward. Continue thus, so when the
mortal who struck down the Giants by plunging into their
backsides the winged shafts of victory, did so only out of
cowardice. Ignore the Olympian chants which they sang in
admiration of his honor: the Nereids and Oceanides casting
rose petals before his feet when Uranus placed upon his
brow the wreath of greatness. Join the four-hoofed
monster's plight of Nessos, who among all the Centaurs,
alone survived Mount Pholoë's slaughtering retribution.

   But no, don't believe Herakles is Zeus' son. Such is
impossible. Herakles is mortal and shall easily perish as a
mortal. I beseech you, never inquire, from the forests of
snow-capped Dirfi, of Euboean importance of whose fame
shall endure in the whispers of the wind: yours, or
Herakles? The breasts whose nipples you tendered will
surely laugh at you.

In the braggarts' Hall of Festivities, do not call Philoctetes or Atalanta cowards for their mastery of the bow. Do not sneer at Artemis with your envious degradation of the bow, for when the spear breaks and the sword shatters, what is left to dissuade the enemy but the sharp eye that can fire innumerable arrows true to their mark?

When chariots tumble over the carcasses of dead horses, and when men run to high-hilled embankments of engorged streams, who but the master archer can fall the enemy while remaining safe at a distance, reducing the ranks of the enemy so the warrior armed with spear and sword may advance without fear. Who but the archer can provide such courage to such warriors?

These recorded facts you cannot debate. Nor, can you justify to me, a reason to execute these three youngsters. To fear the future actions of these offspring, birth by a great warrior, is not justification to murder them. Why bring upon yourself Zeus' inescapable wrath?

LYKUS

Because Hera tasked me to annihilate all of Herakles' family so I may sit upon Kreon's throne. Such ambition, through the smallest kernel of ambition, rose to an achievable possibility. When that idea finally nurtured, it became realized. Now, I am burdened with a debt that must be paid.

AMPHITRYON

Have you not already proven yourself to be proficient, industrious, a master tactician, and a leader among leaders? Therefore, let's unite in a new mission so Zeus may come to love you and despise Hera, enhancing your wealth, power, prestige. King, not only of Thebes, but Athens as well. To do this will require from you the slightest gesture of mercy. Permit my family an easy escape across the Land of Kadmus. The winds of decision are not stout unless it be the true wind of mercy. He, who conquered the Minyans in battle supreme, will avert his eyes when he sees you sitting upon the throne of Thebes. Herakles will not wage war upon you. He will greet you as a friend, and pledge to you his protection for having saved his family from unrecoverable harm.

Should any harm afflict these children, then the shame falls on Hellas as well as on Deucalion and Pyrrha who should have died atop Mount Parnassus rather than repopulate the world with intoxicated mortals lusting solely for self-adorned advancement.

Lykus, I am old, embittered, incapable of defending my grandchildren and daughter-in-law. I implore you to help us. Only my voice can pronounce a reasonable alternative to Hera's scheme.

O how I yearn to be young and strong, to hold again the spear of resolve in my hand, its reconciliation granted on first thrust into my enemy's yellow-haired corpse. Flee then, enemies, beyond the Atlantic Ocean to where Celtics wander in a dismal quest for country, religion, and kingships. Alas, my strength has forsaken me. My muscles ache.

                    LEADER OF THE THEBAN ELDERS
Listen to the brave man's imploring words. In them rest solitude.

                              LYKUS
He speaks and speaks without end. His words beg and yearn for salvation from the devise of Hera's anger as manifested through my actions. His swords: once wondrous and marvelous, will not turn me from my hate-filled path.
                    (To ATTENDANT.)
How I hate whiners. Command my foresters to journey to Mount Helicon where once Pegasus with hardened hoof snapped loose the containing boulder of the Hippocrene spring. From the deep-layered embankments, where Narcissus died of starvation glancing at his exquisite face, cut down a hundred trees and pile them about this Temple where I will offer to the gods these priests and Herakles' family as a sacrifice to my established rulership over the city of Thebes. This consuming fire shall glorify my triumph.

                    LEADER OF THE THEBAN ELDERS
Earthlings divine, how is it you have forgotten our origin? Did not Arês, when the cosmos first glittered with stars, fight the dragon furiously until he conquered it and extract from its powerful vice-clenching jaws, its teeth to spawn upon the universe the greatest race ever to exist? Are we not they? Is not Hellas our home? Are we not the emancipator of stifling authoritarianism upon the globe? Now, lift your staffs and your farming implements into your right hands and strike boldly the mercenaries' heads until they are crushed dead.

Lykus is an usurper: a commoner without credentials who out of greed and malice convinced the newly empowered families to join him in a quest to overthrow the established protectors of Thebes. His youthful callousness

and antisocial behaviors are worse than corruption. He is
the embodiment against the essence of our culture. When has
he ever worked to attain a statesman's respect or earn a
house bespeaking his wisdom? No. He steals what he wants.
Murders those who oppose him. Robs the established order of
their values.

Lykus entered our land cursing our existence.

For this alone, while I live, Lykus shall not destroy
Herakles' gift to the world and to this city: his children.

                              LYKUS
Fool. Herakles perished long ago in a cavern so deep,
even the darkest angels of death stay far away from it. For
ambition's sake he has abandoned his father, wife, and
children. If he does not care for them, why should we? If
he had a general's simple tactical talent, would he have
left your gates open to my mercenaries? Herakles is the
cause of your city's destruction. His neglect as overlord,
his lacking presence in the tower, speak of his incapacity
to lead. That's why he always runs to Eurystheus, escaping
his responsibilities. Because he has abandoned you for a
fool's errand, fires blaze across the outskirts of Thebes.
Perhaps, once, he may have appeared as a hero to you, but
was the army he fought a worthy opponent?

Who can rely on a so-called hero who becomes easily
bored, adventuring wherever, whenever, as long as he wants,
regardless of the consequences he brings upon his resident
country? Your friend and savior is dead. His own vanity
killed him.

Do not view me as your enemy. I am your genuine friend.
Your protector, glorified by Hera herself to raise an army
to free you from Kreon's luxuriant selfishness. Walk away
from this obscene family before my foresters arrive from
the Mount with wagonloads of timbering torches.

                             MEGARA
Fathers of Thebes, Leaders of the People, I thank you for
revealing to me your true characters. My husband's
reputation is wrongfully abused by a heckler bent toward a
loathsome rule. Herakles is in need of bold, faithful
friends in spite of the threatening menace standing before
us. But you, though steadfast, are aged and worn. I
implore, do not step into harm's path.

Amphitryon, listen to me.

I love my sons.

How can I hate those whom I birthed and worked so hard to
protect against the vices of this world? Though I tremble

with fear, still, I will die for those whom I love. But, I will not evade the circumstances afflicting my family. The undeniable reality, though harsh and numbing, will not render me into a helpless dependent. Because our deaths are demanded, then let us die with dignity: without screams or pleads for mercy, and without betraying our friends and family on the hopeless and false promise of a reward.

                    LYKUS
    Die you shall, Megara. First your friends. Second your father-in-law, then when the woodsmen begin running out of wood, prolonging the anguish of burning flesh, your children whose terrible screams will not stop until the smallish flames erupt their hearts from their unimaginable pain. Last, you shall die. A finger burned off. A hand burned off. A toe followed by a foot. Your hair, then your eyes and cheeks. Your breasts last, but never your tongue for every trembling fear you emit, I promise I will forever cherish as I make love to every woman I demand to have. Memories of your supreme anguish will become the elixir of my orgasm.

                    MEGARA
    What makes you think I will scream? No. I will endure every torturous moment, glaring so hard into your eyes, it will be you who absorbs my pain. With every single dying second, I will curse you to a damnation so foul, the hideously dejected Titans will laugh at you as the ugliest thing ever imprisoned in Hades.
    I am the wife of great Herakles, and no matter what you set on doing to me and my family, I will never forsake his honor.

                    LYKUS
    In honor, burn.

                    MEGARA
    So my husband may not totally amputate all your body parts from you through months of lingering agony, allow me the dignity of dressing my sons in clothes of noble black from the chests inside my house.

                    LYKUS
    A double favor? Because you are from a royal family, I will permit both favors.

MEGARA
(To AMPHITRYON.)
He permits it. This foul and detestable snake, in his anxiousness to murder my husband's family, permits it. Such a stupid man I have never met. He thinks he has decreed my execution, but fate has a way of establishing alternate schemes.

(MEGARA and her three children are escorted by several guards off the stage.)

LEADER OF THE THEBAN ELDERS
Though I am regressed in age, I long for one single moment of strength to fight Lykus. Amphitryon, Counselor to Kreon, only you can ward off Lykus' cruelty. With one bold effort strike hard into his horse, and with hopes, he and horse may plunge over the cliffs.

AMPHITRYON
I cannot muster the strength to jump off this altar to breach myself into his horse's side. Yet, do not think I refuse because I am a coward or that I want to keep on living, escaping death's desire to escort me into Pluto's darken enclosure. I still believe, even in this moment of inhospitable impossibilities, that my son will faithfully appear to rescue us.

LEADER OF THE THEBAN ELDERS
It is a useless fantasy. Herakles will not save us. He is dead.

AMPHITRYON
But you have not seen the things I have seen my son perform. Against tremendous odds he triumphed over treacherous impossibilities.

LEADER OF THE THEBAN ELDERS
Rather you jump at Lykus' horse in an attempt to topple him over the edge then forfeit this singular opportunity to act.

AMPHITRYON
Lykus, why keep yourself miserably bored while my daughter and grandchildren are changing their clothes? Entertain yourself by killing me first.

                          LYKUS
Why are you so eager to die?

                       AMPHITRYON
Too many woodsmen are too eager to watch me burn.
Approach closer, and with drawn sword, grace me with the
manner of Kreon's death.

                          LYKUS
Decapitate you? I wonder, do you suppose Kreon felt any
pain? I think I prefer to chop you to pieces, as your
daughter desires for Herakles to kill me. Each stab slowly
pushed in. First through the arms, then through the thighs,
the stomach, then to the edge of the heart, pausing each
time so you'll feel every inch of the minutest penetration
possible. Then just before you breathe your last, I will
hurl you from this altar that you thought a sanctuary, into
the deep crevice, each thump of your screaming body a
tuneful play to my ears.

                       AMPHITRYON
I have no defense against death's depravity. Come
forward. Kill me.
                  (Praying loudly to ZEUS.)
Zeus, hear me. I raised your son as though he were my
own. I forgive you for having taken my wife into your arms
atop my very bed. My anger was needlessly pronounced.
Before Lykus steals from me my last breath, I entrust back
to you the care of your son.

                  (ZEUS appears only to AMPHITRYON as
                  the other actors freeze in whatever
                  position they are in.)

                          ZEUS
This calling for parentage responsibility from me to
Herakles means nothing to me. Megara says I'm Herakles'
father while you say you are his father. For the sake of
peace, for the sake of a good-upbringing, I named you as
Herakles true father, and so you have become the father of
my son. But because you are a mortal and I am immortal, we
can never associate with one another, for you can never be
my friend, nor I yours.
However, as you raised Herakles in the good things of
life and taught him the value of loyalty, I will tell you
now, I have never discarded your grandsons. Though you may
think I am a bestial degenerate with the women whose hearts

I conquered, fathering a thousand sons, I have never let my eyes wander far from your house. I am not ignorant to your plight, and out of love, shall devise a way to save your grandchildren from Lykus.

> (Enter HERA and
> LYSSA.)

HERA
Zeus, my husband and my brother, you don't know how to love anyone. You haven't the slightest idea how to save Herakles' three sons. You provide false hope and in doing so, prove how remarkably dull your cunning is.

LYSSA
Leave us to our devices. Eurystheus has his pet dog, Herakles his Theseus, and I my Lykus who will oversee a grand performance of delightful vengeance.

ZEUS
(Laughing.)
You think?

> (Exit ZEUS, HERA,
> and LYSSA.)
>
> (LIGHTS FADE.)
>
> (CURTAINS.)
>
> (END of SCENE 1.)

ACT 2

Scene 2

SETTING: At Thebes, before the Temple
                                  of Zeus.

AT RISE: The LEADER OF THE THEBAN
                                  ELDERS and his followers
                                  spread around the altar of
                                  Zeus, dressed in translucent
                                  tunics. They begin dancing
                                  gently which eventually turns
                                  violent.)

LEADER OF THE THEBAN ELDERS
Aelion!

FIRST GROUP
Aelion!

SECOND GROUP
Aelion!

ALL
A . a . . . eee . . . li . . . on.

          (Cymbals clash, flutes play, hands
          with spread fingers jettison up
          toward the heavens.)

                                  (Enter several
                                  totally nude women
                                  sounding the dirge
                                  from the left side
                                  of the stage.)

          (The male CHORUS MEMBERS strip off
          their   outer garments, becoming
          totally naked, running off to the
          right side of the stage, still
          dancing.)

          (The   naked   women   also   begin
          dancing.)

NAKED WOMEN / NAKED CHORUS
(Simultaneously.)

Aelion! Aelion!
Listen to this mourning song,
This paean triumphant song . . .
Wake Phoebes . . . wake.

> (A lyre plays. Dancing continues
> from both the right side and left
> side of the stage. The two groups
> merge into each until they form a
> single group in the center of the
> stage.)

Wake Phoebus! Wake.
Listen to the golden plectrum dancing
upon the strings of the lyre.

> (Enter PHOEBES from
> overhead, riding an
> ornate chariot.)

PHOEBES
Your petitions have woken me. Speak.

FIRST GROUP
Prophesy to us, comfort us . . .
Is Herakles alive?
Whether son of Amphitryon or Zeus,
Does he yet breath among the shadows of death?

SECOND GROUP
Phoebes, daughter of Gaea, grandmother of Apollo,
with love divine we praise you
for saving our savior from the
trials of his twelve burdens.
Now allow him his thirteenth victory . . .
Freedom for Thebes.

FIRST GROUP
Freedom for Thebes.

ALL
Freedom for Thebes.

LEADER OF THE THEBAN ELDERS
Phoebes, a garland of glory we offer you!
Herakles, a crown of kingship we offer you.
Accept it so your three princes may inherit your divinity

And rule Thebes in your stead.
Who will not ally with Thebes
When they see three princes dressed in royal purple?

                         PHOEBES
Herakles means nothing to me.

                LEADER OF THE THEBAN ELDERS
Herakles is Hera's most hated enemy. Of all the mortals,
Athena only loves him. You are Athena's greatest friend,
gifted with prophesy, gifted with healing abilities. Help
him so he can help us. Do this, and we will build a great
temple in your honor.

                         PHOEBES
Is he a great warrior? A magnificent king? A trusted
ambassador between Olympus and the Earthlings? Convince me
to assist him. Dance for me his praises.

                LEADER OF THE THEBAN ELDERS
Daughter and sister of the great Olympians,
Listen to the great deeds of Hellas' most renown warrior.

                    (The DANCERS run back to their
                    original places. The female dancers
                    are covered with lions' clothing
                    while the male dancers are armed
                    with shields, spears, bows and
                    arrows. Both groups run to-and-fro
                    enacting the story lines of the
                    LEADER OF THE THEBAN ELDERS.)

   I am pleased to reenact before you, Phoebes, glimpses of
our precious hero's adventures. Even if it is true that he
is dead, nevertheless, his memories shall not perish.

                    (A heavy mist covers the floor.)

                    (Enter naked HERAKLES from the lower
                    levels of the stage directly into
                    the center of the stage. The female
                    dancers surround him, enacting a
                    ferocious dance scene representing
                    the Nemean lion's treacherous
                    strength and cunning.)

LEADER OF THE THEBAN ELDERS [CON'T]

Jealous Eurystheus, king of Tiryns of the Argos Confederate, elder stepbrother of Herakles, grandson of Perseus, the holder of the wager's bet between Hera and Zeus who would next rule Mycenae, aligned himself to Hera's insurmountable rage, forging twelve formidable tasks for Herakles to complete before he could compete for right of rulership.

In the first of twelve tasks, steadfast and untrembling youthful Herakles engaged in furious combat the Nemean Lion, born with an impenetrable leather: spears and arrows bouncing off its armored hide.

With patient endurance Herakles sawed down the gnarled olive tree, shaping from its heart a burled club . . . unbreakable. Face-to-face with the salivating jaws and sharpened claws tearing and slashing forth in rapid offense, Herakles, without a flinch, threw his hardened olive-carved club at the head of the Nemean, rendering it unconscious. With the monster's own claws, Herakles gutted the underbelly of the beast, its tender entrails sacrificed to Zeus. Skinning the garment off the beast, he henceforth wore it as his personal clothing over his own shoulders.

> (The dancers surround Herakles, placing over his shoulders the Nemean lion's fur, all bowing to him, then kneeling down, they extend their right arms outward, praising him. Afterward, they return to their perspective areas and change their costumes to appear as Centaurs. They resume their ferocious dance scene.)

In the second of twelve tasks, the youth, now a young, festive man, adventured to Mount Pelion of deeply forested Thessaly where he engaged in friendship with Chiron the medical teacher of Asklepios and the warrior-trainer of Achilles. The Centaurs, Pholos and Nessos, grieved with envy, consumed too much wine. In drunken bout the twosome challenged Herakles to fight to the death. With his poison-dipped arrows from the blood of the Lernean Hydra, Herakles slaughtered both, then with tears unmitigated, aimed his treacherous arrow at Chiron.

Enraged upon discovering their leader's assassinations, the remainder of the battle-hardened Centaurs, unhesitatingly charged in massive unity against Herakles,

their carcasses falling upon the riverbeds of Thessaly—
the wails of the river Penus unable to drown away the
horrific fright of the dying hunters.

> (The dancers return to their
> perspective areas. One female,
> breasts remaining exposed, changes
> her costume to appear as the
> Cerynian Hind. A few other naked
> female actors walk alongside her to
> support her massive gold-colored
> antlers, where, in unison, they
> attack Herakles. The remaining
> women, costumed as gentle fawns,
> remain in the background, gently
> dancing.)

In the third of twelve tasks, Artemis' loved, Keryneian
raised, hooves of bronze, antlers of pure gold, larger than
a horse, faster than the fastest arrow, boldly strived the
dappled hide Ceryneian Hind, the farmers' land its domain,
feasting wantonly on barley and wheat; stripping the lands
of necessary foodstuffs.

This self-awarding nuisance, for its bold theft of food,
despite its beauty, rallied a cry from the husbandmen to
Eurystheus for a hero born to destroy it.

From the land of Keryneia, through the land of Thrace
Herakles pursued it without pause beyond the Riphean
Mountains, home of the Celtics who had gathered at the
frigid levels of the Alps.

There, as the Hyperboreans gasped at the female deer's
beauty, cunning Herakles captured it during its exhausted
sleep. Herakles, pleased and grateful to the dread huntress
of the forest, Oinoë, broke off its golden antlers,
offering them as a prize adored to her, upsetting the
Arcadian nymph, Artemis.

A wager they sealed, the Ceryneain Hind first to
Eurystheus, and if able to hold on to it, his prize, but if
unable to hold on to it, Artemis pride.

> (The dancers return to their
> perspective areas. Four men
> costumed as dreaded horses stand in
> front of Herakles, challenging him
> as the women exit.)

In the fourth of twelve tasks, tasked to capture Diomedes' flesh-ravaging steeds, Herakles set forth across the Anauros River where he stood in its center recalling the tale of Jason's lost sandal as he gazed at Mount Pelion, determined to feed to the vicious man-eating stallions the body of Diomedes, son of Ares and Cyrene. The foolish leader of the Bistones, unable to defeat Herakles, fell to his poisonous arrows, his flesh consumed by the man-eating monsters . . . leaving behind only Diomedes' tunic and ankles. Tamed at last, Herakles harnessed the four obedient horses, with steel-reinforced bits, to Diomedes' chariot driving them boldly across the silver stream of Hebrus to King Eurysthesus' stalls.

> (The male dancers return to their perspective areas. Only one man is dressed as King Cycnus while the other males are dressed in lords' clothing. The women enter, dressed in elegant Greek tunics. All the dancing actors pay fealty to the king. When the king sees Herakles, he draws out his sword, then suddenly jerks downward in feigned pain, rising up with a poisoned arrow in his chest. The guests gasp, in panic, transforming their dancing from celebration to chaotic movements about the stage, ignoring Herakles' approach to the dead corpse.)

In the fifth of twelve tasks, the pretended master of Mycenae, Eurystheus, ordered his stepbrother to journey across the raging Maliac reefs onward to Amphanae where ruled Cycnus, husband of Themistonoe, daughter of King Ceyx, hated enemy of Zeus.

In heated conflict, bloodthirsty robber Cycnus, standing alongside his father, Ares, faced Herakles. With confidence exaggerated, he flung his weak spear at Herakles, who with a single step glanced its thud off his shield, instantly hurling true his own spear through Cycnus' neck. Enraged Ares, attacking, falls to the ground struck by Zeus' lightning. Thereupon, Herakles' retrieved his spear, shattering Ares' thigh.

(A few male dancers return to their
perspective areas and quickly
spread out a green carpet of grass
while the females place a few apple
trees about the stage. As the
dancers are laying out the stage,
another group of men dress inside a
ferocious looking dragon's costume.
As the dragon stalks forward, a few
dancers spin about a few tree,
falling dead. While this is
occurring, females are softly
singing their thematic song:

Phoebes, daughter of Gaea,
grandmother of Apollo,
with love divine we praise you
for saving our savior from the
trials of his twelve burdens.
Now allow him his thirteenth victory . . .
Freedom for Thebes.)

LEADER OF THE THEBAN ELDERS [CON'T]
     In the sixth of twelve tasks journeyed Herakles to the
daughters of Atlas living in the captivating gardens of
Spain's renowned landscape, home to the all-healing Golden
Apples of the nymphs.
     Nearby Ladon, the hundred-headed swarthy-backed dragon
waited for Herakles' approach. Within the sunrise's cove
came forth Herakles, poisonous arrows drawn and fired,
striking Ladon's center eye. Another poisonous arrow he let
loose, striking Ladon's heart, and with a dreadful fall,
Ladon's upright spires, withered.

FIRST GROUP
(Singing.)
Listen Phoebus!
Listen to the golden plectrum dancing
upon the strings of the lyre.
Phoebes, a garland of glory we offer you!
When we see three princes dressed in royal purple
Standing beside their father, Herakles.

(The dancers return to their
perspective areas and grab long and
wide white and blue sheets,

overlapping each other, imitating
ocean waves.)

LEADER OF THE THEBAN ELDERS
In the seventh of twelve tasks, stout, brave Herakles
challenged the might of the ocean itself, swimming head-
long into the furious waves that threatened to topple the
merchants' vessels. With a firm push left and a firm push
right, and a beating of golden-oak oars against the tidal
waves of destruction, Herakles slammed the roiling clash
into calm submission, quieting the rolls of the scorn-
filled storm.
With opportunity gained, the happy merchants rolled their
heavy-laden vessels to the ports of safety where the hungry
populace eagerly waited for their arrival.

(The dancers return to their
perspective areas, carrying small
sections of a prewired landmass
representing the earth. The dancers
leave the stage as a strong male
actor, representing Atlas, enters.
The prewired landscape is lifted
upward, and with moaning sounds
Atlas pretends to lift the world up.
His moans get louder. Herakles,
overhearing, comes to his rescue.)

ATLAS
For a brief respite, help me. I am weary, hungry.

HERAKLES
What if you try to trick me, leaving the task solely to
me?

ATLAS
Then drop Olympus. Should the dwelling residence of the
gods fall, the death and destruction of grand palaces and
elegant temples will not be held against you, but against
me.

LEADER OF THE THEBAN ELDERS
In the eighth of twelve tasks, trusting, empathetic
Herakles placed his outstretched arms underneath Mount
Olympus' landmass, permitting Atlas one month's respite
from his eternal burden.

Stars and flowers unseen for eons, companions nearly forgotten, celebrated when they saw Atlas' approach, his month-long party a renewal of ideologies and devotion; the immortal's home famed once again from its neglect. And Zeus, brightened by Herakles' gift, stared at the stars, thinking of presenting to the emancipating hero a legacy among the constellations.

> (The dancers return to their perspective areas. The females dress in Amazonian battle armor, armed with swords, shields, and spears. The men dress as Grecian soldiers, also carrying swords, shields, and spears. The men and women wage war against each other, performing dances, intertwining as they battle. Herakles, dressed as a general, proudly walks among the men, looking for Hippolyte to fight so he can steal from her Ares' gift: the Golden Girdle. The Amazon female warriors are also reputed to have a vast quality of gold.)

In the ninth of twelve tasks, cunning, bold, aggressive Herakles, learning from Atlas of vast quantities of gold and emeralds in the Land of the Amazons, placed upon his head the commander's wreath, rallying thousands of adventurous young men from Thebes, Sparta, Athens, Tiryns, Pylos, and Mycenae. Onward to Iolcus the thirty-year old commander marched his assembly of youthful soldiers. Upon Iolcus' shores, the eager seekers of wealth, women, and adventure, built a vast armada, voyaging northeast along the shores of Thrace bordering the Aegean Sea until they reached the Hellespont Strait (Dardanelles Strait). At the entry port the thousands of daring conquerors rested and feasted before entering the surges of the Euxine Sea (Black Sea).

Harsh winds from the inlands of Russia and Ukraine blew into the Grecian sails sending them eastward to the Hellas (Greek) colonies of Amastris, eastward to Trapezus, and far past Phasis, where the Grecian youths, dazzled by tales of Jason and the Argonauts longed to visit Colchis where the descendants of the fiery dragons still lived in the vast forests of the Caucasian mountains where on a morning bright, the soldiers could see the paths leading toward the gates to India, past the Scythian hordes.

Obsessed with reaching the Land of the Amazons, the female children of Ares and Harmonia, Herakles set his fleet to voyage northwest, hugging the coastline until his fleet reached the Strait of Kerch, sailing unafraid into the intensely algae-covered waters of the Maeotian Lake (Sea of Azov). The Island of Tauris (Crimea) rested to the southwest, Russia to the northeast, Ukraine to the northwest, while the prized Land of the Amazons waited for the vast army of Herakles to the extreme north of the Maeotian Lake, the cities of the Amazon Warriors settled beside the Tanais River (Don River).

"Thalatta! Thalatta!" (The Sea! The Sea!) roared the adventurous youths when they encountered the shallow waterways of Maeotian Lake. Upon their entry the warriors lined the edges of their ships, exploring the garfish, the whiting, the dolphins, breams, and the gentle sharks. Wild geese, ducks, cormorants, herons, and sandpipers played among the charales, pond weed, and water lilies of the estuaries leading to the mouth of the Tanais River.

On first landing on the marsh land on his death-fraught quest, Herakles met the fierce and violent Scythians, commanded by Hippolyte, Queen of the Amazons, daughter of Cronos and Rhea. With raised spears and flying arrows, the brutal onslaught commenced, not wavering nor abating until powerful Herakles slammed his shield directly against Hippolyte's breasts, knocking her unconscious. With a swift thrust, he slammed hard his spear through her right breast, killing her. With war cries supreme, the youthful conquerors devastated the Scythian forces, pushing further north, raiding the Amazon cities, taking from them all their gold and precious stones, afterward setting the cities ablaze.

Herakles, with the Golden Girdle wrapped over his shoulder returned home, crossing the coastal lands of Romania and Bulgaria, back through the Sea of Marmara leading to the Dardanelles. While he traveled back home amidst an escort of joyously performing dolphins, a few Greek warriors, curious of what rested further north, adventured through the soil-enriched land, until they discovered the waterways leading to the edges of the Artic.

> (The dancers return to their perspective areas. The male dancers dress as a pack of vicious wolves on the right side of the stage while

> nine women dress as a single Hydra
> on the left side of the stage. From
> the center of the wolves appears
> Herakles armed with a sword and his
> charioteer, Iolaus, carrying a red-
> tipped spear. Flames rise from the
> stage floor. The nine females,
> coordinated as one, face off
> Herakles allowing Iolaus to
> maneuver behind them.)

                    LEADER OF THE THEBAN ELDERS
Aelion!

                              FIRST GROUP
Aelion!

                             SECOND GROUP
Aelion!

                                  ALL
A . a . . . eee . . . li . . . on.

          (Cymbals again clash as the flutes
          resume playing.)

              LEADER OF THE THEBAN ELDERS
    In the tenth of twelve tasks, cautious, aging Herakles,
journeyed to Lake Lerna, near the city of Argos in the Argolid
in the region of Peloponnese, accompanied by his courageous
nephew and charioteer, Iolaus. Across the karstic limestone
landscape the two adventured until they found the Lernaean
Hydra, protected by a herd of ten-thousand wolves.
    Hera's favorite pet, the serpentine sea monster, ruled the
lake without fear, emitting poisonous gas out of its
detestable mouth to unwary fishermen getting too close to its
formidable presence.
    Herakles' nose, covered with a large cloth, fearlessly
steps in front of it, swinging his sword, quickly decapitating
its first head, sending a fright over the wolf pack.
Instantly, Iolaus seared the quivering neck with his iron-
hot spear, cauterizing the wound. A second, third, fourth
time Herakles fought the serpentine monster, each time,
Iolaus searing its wound to prevent two heads taking the place
of one head. On each decapitation the wolf pack cringed,
shimming in fright as it scampered away. Hera, furious at the
wolf-pack's cowardice, sends against Herakles a multi-clawed

crab, its serpent bite filled with poison. Brave, swift-footed Herakles, upon the moment it neared him, laughed at Hera's dismal ploy, crushing the crab without pause in his swings against the Hydra's

A fifth, sixth, and seventh head rolled off the Hydra's serpentine body, each time Herakles laughing at Hera.

> (Enters Lyssa.)

LYSSA
Stop. You have won your victory. Leave Lerna. Return to Thebes where waits Megara and your sons.

HERAKLES
My victory is not yet won. One more head remains: the head of immortality bestowed upon this filth should someone like me fight the beast of anguished terror. Your deceit is useless against me because I have consulted the Oracles before I journeyed on my war-instilled anger.

LYSSA
Hera and I raised him, so show mercy, and I will grant you mercy on the day you most need it.

> (Enter ATHENA. She tosses him her sword.)

ATHENA
With my sword, destroy the Hydra. Let Hera's hate fall upon me.

LEADER OF THE THEBAN ELDERS
With a quick-skilled swing Herakles cuts off the ninth head of the Hydra, its reeling body making it difficult for Iolaus to sear the stump with his iron-hot spear. With a forceful jump and grasp, Heracles stills the Hydra for Iolaus' stinging spear to sear shut the flowing poison. Taking all his remaining arrows, Herakles dips them in the blood of the serpentine, coating the tips with an unremovable poisonous layer.

ATHENA
Beware the Shirt of Nesseus.

> (Exit LYSSA and ATHENA.)

LEADER OF THE THEBAN ELDERS

After setting the serpentine's carcass on fire, Herakles adventured on his eleventh of twelve tasks, confronting the three-bodied, four winged-giant, Geryon. Eurystheus, desiring the extraordinary herd of red-hued cattle feasting off the rich grassland of the last island before the great fall of the waters into the river Styx. This circular body of raging water, Oceanus, Herakles sailed upon to capture for Eurystheus, the renowned red-hued cattle alive for his barns.

Three battles he waged to gain the herd. First, destroying the two-headed dog, Orthros, who patrolled the perimeter. Second, terminating the life of the herdsman, Erythaean. Finally, Herakles slew with one arrow, to the center of his forehead, Greyon, in mid-flight.

Innumerable tasks Herakles accomplished, always victorious in his quests to serve humanity.

Now, Phoebes, even as Athena has helped Herakles with her own sword, will you help Herakles escape from Hades into whose darkened caverns he adventured into with Theseus to tame Cerberus?

Will you help his children avert the crossing from life into death, and render useless their journey over the dank river upon Charon's boat? Should they cross, for all of Herakles' pleads and the priests' prayers, not one shall ever return to life, not one to smile again upon the faces of his mother and father.

Phoebes, if I were young and strong, I would venture into the center of Hades and call upon Herakles' name to lead him out those treacherous tunnels to the light of the world. Quick, help us, as I see walking toward us Megara and her three sons, prepared for the sacrificial fire of eternal consumption.

PHOEBES

I will think about it after talking to Athena.

                              (Exit PHOEBES and
                              all the dancers.)

LEADER OF THE THEBAN ELDERS

Among all the gods of Olympus, is there not one of you willing to help Herakles? To help us? O how I grieve in such remorseful anguish knowing all has been for naught, and for naught I lived.

(Exit ALL.)

(LIGHTS FADE.)

(CURTAINS.)

(END OF SCENE 2.)

ACT 2

Scene 3

SETTING: At Thebes, before the Temple
                                 of Zeus.

AT RISE: Enter MEGARA, AMPHITRYON, and
                                 CHILDEN.

MEGARA

Evil is a terrible conductor. It carries no remorse, for
it has no heart. It plots harm every second of every day:
to cripple you, to steal from you, to destroy your
reputation, to abuse you . . . to degrade you in any manner
whatsoever it desires. Evil can never be modified, nor
reshaped. Evil is a lusting force bent on malice, and
malice it shall have.

Where can we turn for peace, tranquility, equality? Never
to the priest. Their intercessions are fallacious, filled
with the worm wood of deceit, seeking not grace, but
painful intercourse as they steal from you your coinage in
exchange for an empty prayer. They ply your mind with
things soft while they tear your heart into fractious
maladies within the artful tune of a rhyme. They have no
stars in the cosmos, no heroes. They are a collection of
ill-bred contemptuous freaks thinking only of their own
gain. I hate all priests for they murder your soul while
they kiss your lips.

Tell me, priest, are you the one who will light with the
torch the pile of kindling wood beneath my feet? Will you
laugh as I scream in terror? Will you lust after my naked
flesh when the flames discard my robe, showing you for a
fleeting moment amply grown breasts?

Will you, priest, comfort my three children with
fantasies and lies of Uranus, Hera, Athena as they step
upon the piles of dry wood? Will you tell them stories of a
chariot made from gold with the purest white stallions
pulling their innocent graces through the heavens so all
may adore them as they pass by?

Priests and haruspices, have you prepared for yourselves
lying scripts for mothers, fathers, children, brothers and
sisters? What sheep liver can tell the truth: divisions and
lines crisscrossing of veins and muscles in pretensive
abundance accidentally matured.

I am helpless. Doom waits impatiently for me.

Terror grasps for my children's hands.

My children, my dear children whom I nurtured with my breasts, for what did I bring you into the world? To face false accusers who would for self-entertainment abuse you? There are men in this world who will betray you in a thorough deceit, saying one thing, meaning another: scoffing your last moments in a drunkard's den. You sons have no meaning to such men. You are functionaries of pleasure set to be destroyed.

Children, this world has shattered my dreams of deeply harbored hopes of your rise in this world to change it to a better thing for friends, family, country, and God.

These grievances and shames rip against my heart.

I trusted your father's promises to build for us a fine house, with honor and prestige set to our names. With assured fame he should have stopped his adventures, but no, one final time, one last adventure, one needed deed to create a better and safer world, he said to me, convincing me to kiss his lips as he and Thebes descended into the craggy sharp cliffs of Hades into the bowels of death where waited Lyssa, Iris, and Hera.

I wonder, children, if you still remember Eurystheus' palace where we were promised residence, eternal? Do you remember the wondrous landscapes of Pelasgia, whose fragrance swayed our bodies with delicious intoxication?

I wonder if my children remember the day their father cast off the Nemean lion's fur from his shoulders, and wrapped it about their three bodies, who combined from should-to-shoulder, could not muster a fraction of strength to hold it in place.

Hera has cheated you, dear husband, of allocating to our three children their inheritance.

O children, children, your inheritance has been stolen, your wealth gifted to Lykus by Hera's treachery.

Therimachus, prime inheritor of Argos, designated occupier over the House of Eurystheus, master over the vast productive lands of Pelasgian. This spring-fed farmland, filled with vast herds of cattle and sheep, where the gnarled olive trees thrive and where innumerable acreage of barley grow, such an inheritance has been forfeited to you by an adventurer's fantasy. In your hand, Therimachus your father entrusted the Mace of Defense to protect your people and inheritance. Now, instead of guarding yourself against Daedalus' false wiles, it is Lykus' flames in which you must be afraid.

To you Deicoon, your indisputable reign over Thebes was approved by the Gods themselves. Oh how your father longed to have his prime horses swiftly-pulling his chariots through the wide avenues of marble. How he longed to have you mandate for Thebes to hold monthly festivals where a champion's talent could challenge insurmountable Herakles' skills.

Creontiades, to you, the youngest, your father set aside the village of Oechalia, which by his own hand he conquered, striking down King Eurytus who had dared to lie to your father, making a false promise of giving to the victor of an archery contest his daughter's hand, beautiful Iole. After your father won the challenge, the king refused, saying he was already married to me, but I never protested, knowing he engaged in the challenge solely to secure for you an inheritance. Iole waits for you in Athens, but now she will be set free to marry Lykus: an imprisonment far worse than the concubine bed of my aged husband. O what other woman could be more generous to her husband than I: tolerant, never jealous, obedient, serving his passion as a dutiful wife should lovingly do.

How I dreamed of seeing you three growing into manhood, the designated rulers over Hellas' greatest cities: Athens, Thebes, and Sparta. From Herakles the establishment of a Grecian world united, your unification anchored throughout the world, assuring you a happy life.

O children, if only you could have known the great excitement that Atlas enflamed in your father's heart, the ambition he stirred over Herakles as he held upon his own shoulders Mount Olympus. His march against the Amazons took hold on him a realization of a united Grecian empire ruling the world as one: Hellas, eternal.

Now, all those dreams are cast aside, waiting for the arrival of another who may also gain the spark of ambitious unification: one country, one language, one government.

Fate is a fickled bride. My tears, though heavy, will not be permitted to fill the bathing tubs of the brides. Your marriages and kingdoms have been shattered through the devious folly of Hera who can not fathom the ultimate nature of men to live in harmonic balance. No, she prefers Lykus' fragmented cities, while Zeus cares only for his own sexual gratification.

It is impossible for anyone to visualize the depths of anguish which I suffer, not because I am about to die, but because I dream dreams impossible. To whom, in this desperate cycle of life, can I turn to for help? My husband is dead. He whose naked flesh adorned my naked flesh, perished in a land so distant, I can only wonder at the callousness of his desire to leave his family to their uncertain future. I can never again embrace him. I carry with me only glimpses of his face. As a honey bee once joyous to be filled with nectar from the fields of glee, now only exist the torrid flowers of poisonous grief.

O Herakles, Herakles, listen to my solitary cry.

I love you. I love you.

Ghosts and wandering spirits, send my message to my dearest husband: I love you.

Tell him how desperate my need is for him. His father is about to be murdered by the cruel devices of an envious evil as are his children and wife.

If you cannot save us, so be it. Wife my dying last breath I say to the world, "I bless my husband with all my heart."

(LIGHTS FADE.)

(CURTAINS.)

(END OF SCENE 3.)

ACT 2

Scene 4

SETTING: At Thebes, before the Temple
                                      of Zeus. Piles of kindling
                                      wood is stacked nearby, with
                                      two guards holding torches.

AT RISE: Enter AMPHITRYON.

                              AMPHITRYON

Theses aged and worthless bones are finished living. You,
woman, continue lowering your eyes to Hades and absorb
yourself in useless pity, for what you had hoped to be a
future bright and prosperous is never guaranteed to happen.
Life for me—for us, for now— is a life facing extinction. I
shall not look to hell's damnation, but rather I shall look
for a heavenly entry. Shall I reach heaven I promise to
petition Zeus for your children's salvation.

Set your mind on a dignified death so you will not wail
when you face it. Think of old friends and good times
shared. Life's span is brief. Live it as happily as you
can. Do not waste your waking hours from sunrise to sunset
moaning and grieving and desiring alternatives that are not
there, for nothing can avert time's demise nor create a
direction unattainable. Nothing can lengthen our hours.
Work swiftly in your tasks. Do not delay in your efforts.

Fate and destiny have taken from everyone a full expanse,
so observe that your manners are well balanced and
beneficial. Our souls will drift as a feather
directionless, if we do not enhance our living breaths
with purpose divine.

I have never met a wealthy man so generous he will share
during times of illness and distress his entire estate to
assure himself a famed renown of love. No, only those who
had suffered through deep anguishes are capable of
tendering others.

Megara, farewell. Farewell to he who was our best friend.

May all my friends be happy in the remainder of their
years.

Look upon me as a friend who smiled definitely at death's
theft.

(Exit.)

(LIGHTS FADE.)

(CURTAINS.)

(END OF SCENE 4.)

ACT 2

Scene 5

SETTING: At Thebes, before the Temple
                                      of Zeus. Piles of kindling
                                      wood is stacked nearby, with
                                      two guards holding torches.

AT RISE: Enter HERAKLES. The CHORUS
                                      rallies forward with a brisk
                                      dancing as cymbals and flutes
                                      happily play.

                    LEADER OF THE THEBAN ELDERS
Aelion!

                         FIRST GROUP
Aelion!

                        SECOND GROUP
Aelion!

                             ALL
A . a . . . eee . . . li . . . on.
Aelion! Aelion!
Listen to this triumphant song:
Athena has stirred Phoebes' heart.
Phoebes wakes with purpose firmly resolved!

                              (Exit ALL.)

                         HERAKLES
                    (Enthusiastically.)
    Greetings members of my house and citizens of Thebes.
Greetings! How happy I am to see all of you! I have
returned from the dank darkness of hell to gaze upon you
again with love.
                    (Suddenly realizes the plight of his
                    family.)
    But wait! Wait!
    What am I seeing? Not running children with merriment in
their hearts to touch a father long absent from home.
NO! NO! I see my children captured as prisoners wearing
upon their bodies death's attire with mourning wreaths atop
their shaved heads.

Why is my wife surrounded by the priests of Thebes and soldiers standing about with flaming torches in their hands?

Why is my father crying so bitterly? Are they mourning my demise though I live? Or, has Kreon, my friend, prematurely perished? I need to know what has happened.
                    (HERAKLES runs up to the altar,
                     pushing aside the guards who formed
                     up in front of him.)
Wife, what is this strange gathering of priests and soldiers? Has something grave afflicted a cherished servant of my house or one of my friends?

                         MEGARA
                 (Collapsing into his arms as she
                  laughs and cries simultaneously.)
O dearest husband, how is it you have so miraculously appeared to us when we need you the most? Suddenly, from out of nowhere, you are here.

                         HERAKLES
How? I don't know how. One hour I was walking near the seashore, the next moment, I find myself in front of you.
                    (To AMPHITRYON.)
Father, why is there so much clamor here? Who has died to arouse such a commotion? Kreon? A favorite servant? One of your best friends?

                        AMPHITRYON
Son, such an answer from my lips will enrage you to a feverishly danger. Allow Megara to answer.

                         MEGARA
Husband, Kreon was hideously murdered as were all our servants and all our friends. Thousands of men, women, and children throughout Thebes have been needlessly slaughtered . . . annihilated through the sheer chaos of greed's vanity.

We are the last of loyal Thebans, our rights taken away through the willing participation of anarchy's power. For loyalty, our lives are set to perish through the flames ignited from our own forests.
                    (Breaks down crying.)
Forgive me my plight of tears. Women are swift to feel the burden of grief. I thought myself and my children doomed, my eyes alighting solely on the fires of hatred ignited.

                         HERAKLES
Apollo! What am I hearing? What am I seeing?

                          MEGARA
All our friends and servants are dead. Murdered.

                         HERAKLES
Why? They have never harmed anyone. Tell me who carried
the slaughtering spear.

                          MEGARA
Lykus the merchant killed them. Lykus, the usurper. He
and his conspirators now rule seven-gated Thebes. Now, from
beneath the caverns of inescapable hell, appears you to
avenge us. These eyes that have for so long yearned to see
you before I die, am satisfied. Hurry now, dearest husband,
dearest love, and strike dead Lykus and all his cohorts!

                         HERAKLES
I still don't understand why Lykus wanted to murder you
and my children? What was he afraid of?

                          MEGARA
He feared the future. Having slain Kreon, he imagined
that one day one of our three sons may, in turn, murder
him. For his callous fear, Lykus demanded our children to
be attired in the black shrouds of death.

                         HERAKLES
How is it he had the daring to murder you through such
violent a means as burning?

                          MEGARA
Friendless, who opposed him? Worse, the heralds of your
stepbrother, Eurystheus, endorsed the cruel method of our
deaths.

                         HERAKLES
Forgive me, I just don't understand this treachery. I
need to reconcile my mind with these occurring events. I
don't understand how Lykus overwhelmed my posted guards to
drag you to this altar without resistance. I need to
understand why Lykus dared to assault the man who raised
and protected me. Why did Eurystheus permit this without
raising an alarm and swiftly dispatching his best troops to
protect my family?

                              MEGARA
    Ask those questions to Hera, the manipulator and crafty
designer of this hideous plot.

                             HERAKLES
    Hera? Who else but Hera. How I wish I had bitten off her
entire breast and fiercely kicked my foot into her vagina.
Thus, Eurystheus, my stepbrother for whom I labored so
wearily, forsook my family by bribing the guards to vacant
my premises, leaving my family unprotected against Lykus'
bold plot. Whatever true friends I had are now dead, and
the untrue friends who pretended admiration and
congratulations, feast in falsely earned monies. I am a man
beset by terrible misfortunes.

                              MEGARA
    Stop questioning why these things happened and set your
mind to avenging us. Rally forward a thirteenth time and
destroy he who sought to destroy you.

                             HERAKLES
    So easy to say. Megara, you see before you a semblance of
a man grown weary, fraught with pain in his legs,
shoulders, and arms. I no longer wear the lion's suit
because it is too burdenous for me to carry. I no longer
walk with a shield as I can barely balance it in my arm as
I wield the sword. I rely on my bow and arrows, for they
alone, but who knows for much longer, have sustained me
through the years, winning for me countless victories. In
the eyes of the spearsmen, in the eyes of the sword-
wielder, I am a coward reliant on a safe distance to
survive and overwhelm my pursuers. I have heard the
talkers, and the talkers are correct. The overt and covert
rumors have not lied. I am too weary to go on fighting
beasts, warrior women, and innumerable odds. I am here, so
let us go to another city. Let us find refuge in
mountainous Crete.

                              MEGARA
    You will not leave Thebes without first killing Lykus and
all his men. If there be ten, a hundred, a thousand, you
will kill each and every one of them, regardless how much
your pain-filled and suffering agony afflicts you. Look at
your children who wear the black vestment of death. Look at
me who barely escaped being raped and torn to pieces. Look
at your father who was nearly crippled and tortured. You,
who had labored twelve times for a betraying brother, will

now labor a thirteenth time to restore dignity to his family. My children will grow up to be men of courage as exemplified by their father and world uniters who will make Hellas the master country of all cities throughout earth: east, west, south, and north, for you have shown them the paths to all countries.

HERAKLES
You have no understanding of how gravely the monsters and wandering spirts found all the fears contained and subverted inside me while I fought in the caverns of Hades. Never have I been so frightened. I battled against Hera and came face-to-face with Lyssa, fighting shield against flame, spear against magic, life against death. Should I lose my next battle, Pluto will assuredly place in in the front center of all my enemies where I will endlessly fight without rest or compassion, suffering the hacking off of my arms and legs, and, similar to Prometheus, wake each day with restored limbs only to have them viciously amputated again. No. I want to leave this wretched city and settle in tranquil Crete.

MEGARA
You will not do this shameful thing to me. The priest danced and sang throughout the night, waking Phoebes to endow you with the strength of a million warriors. You will not lose the fight against Lykus. You will triumph, and in so doing, create the most formidable family to ever exist, ruling for ten-thousand years united Hellas.

HERAKLES
Perhaps this is why so many Olympians hate me? One world. One government must surely frighten them. Mankind serving one ruler, one assembly, harmonious in aspect, balanced in the welfare of each other. Strife will be removed. The gods will lose their purpose if they cannot manipulate one nation to hate another nation.
All the reason for us to get away from Thebes. Remove from your head the burial garments. It is time to look forward to living in the light of peace. Quick, let's go to Crete.

MEGARA
My husband the coward of cowards.

HERAKLES

You don't understand the suffering I underwent. I need peace more than I need a wife, more than I need children, more than I need a father: or status, or wealth. I need to get away from this world and find solitude. I have reached the breaking point of my endurance.

MEGARA

Fight, I tell you. Fight. Do not leave this city without first killing Lykus. I demand it for the right of my honor's sake. For the right of your children's sake. For the right of prosperity, I demand you to fight.

HERAKLES

I WILL NOT! I WILL NOT!

(He runs off. MEGARA chases after him, slapping him hard when she catches up to him.)

MEGARA

I don't care what frightens you as much as it does. I don't care how much suffering and misery you experienced in the caverns of Hades. I don't care about anything except for my restored dignity.
(She slaps him again.)
If I had a sword, I would kill you for betraying me; wanting to run away from expected duty. As your wife, I am entitled to your life. I permitted you concubines, whores, drunken bouts, and I never denied you a single adventure. Now you come home after my shamed degradation in front of all Thebans and tell me you want to live a peaceful life in Crete. You worthless animal, whose father's name you don't even know. Go to Crete. Find a hole. Buy a whore. Drink yourself to death, miserable coward.

HERAKLES

From the nether-gloom I rose seeking a wife's tender embrace, a house of warmth filled with loving children and a father respecting his son. Instead, I find myself inside the workings of a thirteenth labor unexpected, imported to this land through the cunning of Eurystheus obeying the incessant whispers of Hera.
Poor Lykus, my enemy to die through no fault of his own.

MEGARA

Will you avenge me, or must I go to the Spartans?

HERAKLES
Yes, I will murder men for you. And, why shouldn't I?
Noble dignity demands for me to raze Lykus' house and
annihilate all his soldiers.

MEGARA
Not annihilate. Not exterminate. But, decapitate as they
had Kreon.

HERAKLES
Cerberus is not here for me to feed him their heads. The
Hydra no longer exists for me to feed them their heads. The
carnivorous horses no longer live, to feed them their
heads. Tell me, will you consume their heads?

MEGARA
With absolute delight I will sup on their carcasses. I
and the feral dogs.

HERAKLES
Where is my battering ram shaped from the trunk of the
olive tree?

MEGARA
Inside your home underneath the Nemean Lion's fur.

HERAKLES
Under your command, I will fill high the Ismenus with
their corpses. One hundred, or a thousand, I will slaughter
them as though they were one. Dirkê's crystal clear waters
will turn red with blood.

MEGARA
Had you not left us, you would not now be in this
predicament.

HERAKLES
After I finish killing all your enemies, how will you
cope with me? I tell you, I suffer grave nightmares that
incapacitate my abilities as a warrior. My manhood is shorn
as I tremble in the night, seeing time-after-time the
ghosts of my past. I am afflicted. I have no cure for it.

MEGARA
Violence release will cure you. Now, go, Herakles the
Victorious.

HERAKLES
I am past fifty, and at this age still I fight the
impossible fight. May Athena and Apollo calm my reproach
after I have destroyed these thousand men who had
threatened my family. Peace is not my destiny. Fate
regurgitates at such a notion. No. I will die in tortured
pain, inflicted upon me by my own wife.

                              (Exits.)

                              (LIGHTS FADE.)

                              (CURTAINS.)

                              (END OF SCENE 5.)

ACT 2

Scene 6

SETTING: On the road to HERACLE'S
                                  house.

AT RISE: Enter the PRIEST, AMPHITRYON,
                                  and HERAKLES.

PRIEST

Do not be afraid. The gods of Olympus anoint you with
this killing task. Your wife has issued to you a lawful
command, a rightfully placed demand. Her suffering requires
purification of her enemies so she may sleep without
burdensome fright.

HERAKLES

Why is it no one accepts my own trepidations? Every night
I wake up with sweat on my brow. My hands shake. My body
quivers. I suffer from too many regretful encounters. It
will only take a spark during my sleep to set me off into
an untamed fury where I will do that which must never be
done. Look, even now my hands shake with fear. I want no
part of this coming bloodshed. Priest convince my wife to
accompany me to Crete.

AMPHITRYON

Son, you, among all men, were born for this fight. Let it
be your crowning achievement. Your victory will bring
flocks of friends to your doorsteps, each bearing gifts of
praise. Determine in your heart to hate Lykus and his
cohorts. They are your mortal enemies, sworn to kill you no
matter where you go. Crete, the newly discovered Artic
region, to the farthest eastern lands beyond India or the
western most lands beyond Spain. Lykus' men will hunt you
down and they will kill you. Caution and fear will wear you
out. Exhausted, you will fail, and in your failure, suffer
a most vile death.

HERAKLES

Even so, your rashness surprises me. Is it courage that
drives you forth to kill, or some other reason?

                              AMPHITRYON
     Lykus the merchant has forged many treaties with
countless cohorts. They steal what they want when they
want, enriching themselves without end. But to what
purpose? The gold is spent faster than it is stolen. They
surround themselves with lavish parties as they bind other
citizens to their cause. Sedition runs amuck throughout
this land.
     Should we save this city, it will be an impoverished and
ruined population we encounter. It behooves you to set the
dire of Thebes straight.

                               HERAKLES
     I find it strange. I ride forward, armed with shield,
spear, sword, bow and arrows, my best weapon, a reputation
fearsome; yet not one single citizen rallies behind me.
Thebes has become an ominous place for me. An evil bird
follows us. A spying bird. It sets a trap for me.

                              AMPHITRYON
     Then I advise you not to stir this city for who knows on
which side the populace fights?

                               HERAKLES
     I will listen to you.

                              AMPHITRYON
     Really? Since when have you ever listened to anything I
said? Son, did you truthfully descend into Hades' caverns?

                               HERAKLES
     Even deeper than I expected. Though I fought monsters and
powerful armies, never have I battled against gods. It took
all my skills to survive that encounter. As I escorted the
three-headed hound out to the chamber of light, my mind was
filled with weeks of countless screams of raging furies.
All the Minyans I killed, all the Amazons I claimed victory
over, all the warriors I subverted, their voices came
rushing to my ears, mercilessly. The orgies of the mystics
weakened me. Even now I walk with their bitterness inside
my mind.

                              AMPHITRYON
     You vanquished all your enemies, protected by Zeus and
Athena. There are no voices afflicting you. If there are,
silence them.

PRIEST

Perhaps a mysterious preparation alerts you to the coming fight. How long were you in Hades?

HERAKLES

Far too long. Theseus, much to my sorrow, was captured. I was duty-bound to rescue him. I wandered from chamber to chamber until I found him, chained and tortured in the lowest center of Hades.

PRIEST

Where is he? Buried in a fine tomb in Athens? Or, did you abandon him in the depths of his miserable outcries in Hades? Is this why you are so conflicted at this time? A guilty conscious?

HERAKLES

I never ran away from my promises. As I took the three-headed dog to Eurystheus, something kept telling me the dog, as misshapen as he is, as unnatural as he is, did not deserve to be tormented by my stepbrother. So I turned to the sanctuary of Chthonia near the city of Hermion to safeguard him.

PRIEST

I heard you killed Cerberus. If so, how could he be safe in Hermion?

HERAKLES

Safe, dead, both versions could be correct. My mind plagues me with double versions. My lies seem truthful and my truths sound as if lies. I should have not come back for Megara and the children. I should have made my way to Crete, and there, live in one world or in another: either world or both worlds, my enrapturing void to all things.

PRIEST

So you would have your family die for an escape to oblivion?

HERAKLES

If I had consumed lotus flowers, what regrets could I experience? Priest, imminent doom is our fate. Men's hearts are treacherous just as much as they are loving. Thebes now lives in comfort in Athens, and how I wish I lived in Crete in comfort.

Fathers love their children until they grow up and rebel and cast the father' aside. Mothers cling to the sons' tunics as they seek a bride. We are all the same, separated only by the things money can buy.

Here I am now, without an army to command, riding headstrong to my fated doom accompanied by an irreligious priest and a cunning old man who thinks himself my father.

(Exit ALL.)

(LIGHTS FADE.)

(CURTAINS.)

(END OF SCENE 6.)

ACT 2

Scene 7

SETTING: On the road to HERACLES'
                                  house.

AT RISE: Enter the LEADER OF THE
                                  THEBAN ELDERS.

LEADER OF THE THEBAN ELDERS
   A vision of unorthodox magnitude's triumph in the spirit
of men marches before us. A fifty-year old warrior dressed
in full armor accompanied by a seventy-five year old man
armed solely with a spear. Though their youth has long
expired, it means nothing to the two courageous warriors
who march in the brilliance of their belief that their
quest is eternally harmonized to defeat evil.
   Such a belief weighs heavily upon my shoulders: heavier
than trying to catch in my arms the far flung boulders of
Mount Etna's fiery explosions. I must flee from this sight
for it calls me to testify to the Court of Jesters that I
saw two determined men, drastically aged and bent, riding
forth with stern faces fixed upon a mission irretractable.
Please cover my eyes with a brown cloth to blind myself so
I can no longer testify of the gloom and doom that I
behold.
   Veiled, new visions impact me. I once dreamt of Persian
gold and India rubies, my treasure chest filled with
emeralds openly strewed upon a desert's dune. But today, I
would refuse to touch the largest jewel in exchange for my
youth. Antiquity is dark, cruel, lonely. The youth of
vitality and discovery transforms into a core of
indistinguishable events hastening toward death.
   Which hateful muse conceived the brain's failure, the
lungs inability to breath, the bending of the shoulder, the
stomach's pouch too engaging in another man's conversation,
the greying, the loss of hair all detriments to the
exuberance of a morning run along the shores of continuing
waves. Drowning has been termed a gentle death. Shall I
then drown myself beneath the next storm's crashing of
waves upon the rocky crags? Why cannot I just softly close
my eyes and let the eagle's shadow ride over me, its wings
carrying me to a place where my eternal spirit can find
comfort? Mistreat me, and after my erasure from green
meadows, my ghost shall haunt your home and village.

All gods are selfishly inclined toward doing anything they can to gain from human beings exclusive applause. Jealousy thrives among the gods, whether good or evil, each contesting against the other to fill up the arena of popularity.

Envious gods, what happened to your wisdom, if ever you had it? The sons of the earth need your guidance. I long to hear a consoling speech and feel the breath of assurance on my cheeks.

Confess to me: are there two stages of life: two cycles of youth? The first, the youth of mortal time limitation, where sinews and flabby arms refuse to hold the lightest stick? It is an ugly existence. Furrows deep, wrinkles abounding, legs seared of strength, a walking resemblance of lost times where a worn and toothless mouth can only jabber incomprehensibilities. The second, a rising from death with flesh youthfully covering the skeleton of eternal life. A body filled with restorative lungs, heart, kidneys, and a brain exceeding the intellect of the gods. In such an existence of purity, will the same sun rise and set upon our new lives? Will this same earth house us? Will the former graves become plowing fields where gigantic squash and melons thrive?

One life lived filled with the disgusting attacks on the body, evil and calamitous, will they continue on in the other life? Will mankind born anew compete for wealth and status? Will the sailing ships know where they are going upon a calm surface, or will they suffer through gale and storm, crashing upon limestone abutments?

Will the flute players and cymbal masters still grace our ears with wondrous compositions and dancers spin and tumble, the characters of the stage manifesting moral themes through reenactments of heroes set upon an impossible quest? Or, in renewed life, will we sit and stare at one another, uncertain how honestly we can declare our words before we reach the one word too impaling, resulting again in malice?

I don't know if I can exist without music. I don't know if I can bear to live eternally without hearing a poem or reading a scroll of a grand adventure.

Worse, will I have to give up drinking my wine and must I cease celebrating joyously to life lived: the seven-stringed lyre my emotional release as the Libyan pipes reveal the interior layers of hidden emotions.

In life renewed must I never again dance? Never gaze upon the firm breasts of Delian girls. Hum a tuneful melody?

If this is secondary life of an eternal youth-filled
existence then I prefer to age hard, knowing I had ventured
on a mighty quest to slay the monster.

Ride forward Herakles, straight and bold. Prove to all
Thebans you are the rightful son of Zeus. Glory awaits you
in this thirteenth labor, your greatest triumph to come.
Leave behind divine direction, for its intercourse has
wavered upon the field where the scions sing their swan-
songs to your glories.

Your feats have gloried the essence of man, made us a
valuable commodity in the face of all Olympian gods. You
alone are capable of stepping forth into the arena of
charging demons intent on murdering you, and walk out
singing your own praise. Slay Lykus and his cohorts. Free
us from his evil. A garland is in my hand, prepared with
the fragrance of Grecian glory.

Hellas, land of your birth. Hellas, the civilizer of
barbarism.

(Exit.)

(LIGHTS FADE.)

(CURTAINS.)

(END OF ACT 2.)

ACT 3

Scene 1

SETTING: Outside LYKUS' palace.

AT RISE: Enter HERAKLES and
                                  AMPHITRYONE.

HERAKLES
Though I am armed heavily with the implements of war,
master of wielding the sword, launching spears and
javelins, unrivaled in the usage of bow and arrows, still I
hesitate to battle Lykus. There is something amiss,
something lingering, something beseeching me not to fight.
I dread the consequences, not of failure, but of victory. I
believe I hear warnings from Athena and Apollo to turn away
from this quest.

AMPHITRYON
The Priest has anointed your revenge. It is a holy quest
performed under the grace of the gods.

HERAKLES
(Sarcatically.)
Sanctified to amputate arms, disgorge intestines, rip
open cheeks. and cut viciously men's chests. Sanctified
under god's decree to murder.

AMPHITRYON
Yes, a warrior gloried to march under the protecting arms
of Zeus to render, make straight, and restore Thebes back
to its missed dignity under divine decree. How many
warriors have achieved this anointing?

HERAKLES
This anointing decree shall become my curse. Knowing
this, I implore you, father, to talk to Lykus to find a
peaceful solution for him to leave Thebes. I will not harm
him if he leaves. But, if he determines to stay, I will not
have mercy on him. Go. Consult with Lykus while I wait
here, reflecting.

                    (Stage lights dim over HERAKLES as
                    he removes his armor.)

                    AMPHITRYON
            (Banging his spear on the door.)
    Give entry to an old man who wishes only to talk peace
with Lykus.

            (The doors open.)

                            (Enter LYKUS.)

                    LYKUS
    Amphitryon, I heard you had thrown away your mourning
garments for a warrior's armor. I see it is true. But why
you delayed to kill me, mystifies me. Had it been me, I
would have rushed for the kill, not linger and pause. Is it
because you're so old your feet barely carried you here?

                    AMPHITRYON
    You are dressed in Kingly robes, but no matter how
elegantly you appear to your cohorts, to me, you are still
an usurper. A merchant using his trading instincts to
thwart the will of the people. But, it no longer matters
what I think of you. Mercy and compassion are offered to
you and your cohorts.
    I pray to god you refuse. I pray to god you will fight
rather than surrender, for I long to slowly insert this
spear through your stomach, focusing my eyes directly on
your speechless eyes, your gapping mouth a sinister joke.

                    LYKUS
    So, the priests found courage in their veins to free you,
Megara, and Alcmena's sons. Where did the priests hide
them? Athens? Sparta?

                    AMPHITRYON
    No. She's at home, attending her children's welfare.

                    LYKUS
            (Laughing.)
    At home, you say? What is she thinking? That I will not
invade her home and this time, rather than waiting for the
fires to enflame her, not kill her where she stands?

                    AMPHITRYON
    The altar steps are for the living. The dying have no
need to sit upon holy ground.

LYKUS

Thus living, she must have prayed hard to sway the
priests to set her free.

AMPHITRYON

Did you not once say to the world that her husband,
Herakles is nothing more than a coward, hiding at a
distance using bow and arrows to gain his fame? Did you not
once say to the world how useless he launches a spear,
always missing his mark, and his sword is nothing more than
a clumsy performance, slashing at best, empty air? A
pretended hero. A falsifier of deeds. An exaggerated liar.

LYKUS

Your memories are too generous. Herakles is the most
incompetent coward ever to walk on the face of the earth.
If he had truly descended into Hades, surely his stupidity
resulted in him becoming forever lost inside its
innumerable caverns. Pluto laughs at his clumsy attempts to
find a passage out of there as Charon yawns from his bored
sitting at the oars.

AMPHITRYON

Just to be sure, before I leave your house, do you accept
or refuse my offer of peace? You can leave Thebes
unmolested. Take with you all your gold. Take with you your
cattle, sheep, and goats. Take with you whatever quantity
of grains, oil and wine that you can load atop your wagons.
Do this now, otherwise all the orange and black shadows
depicted on the amphoras, kantharos, and pithos jars will
depict the true evil shamed.

LYKUS

You are bold. I don't hear the sounds of an armed army in
front of my palace. The sky still shines blue, so Zeus has
not descended with his legions against me. No. I only hear
Hera's comforting words that I am the legal ruler of
Thebes. More, I feel Lyssa's kiss on my lips that I am an
immortal, immune to death. I only see you: a decrepit
seventy-five-year old man who can barely stand in front of
me. Your body weaves so much I merely need to blow hard on
you to make you fall down. I tire of you, so leave me and
return to Megara while you still can. Before I empty my
wine cup, your entire family shall be dead.

                    AMPHITRYON
Before you commence on your murdering spree, look outside
your window. Tell me who the man is asleep on the ground,
having no fear whatsoever of you or your one-thousand
cohorts.

                    (Lykus   walks   to   the   window
                    overlooking Thebes.)

                    LYKUS
I see another aged man, naked, sleeping, on top of a pile
of rusted metal for his bed.

                    AMPHITRYON
Who you see is Herakles.

                    LYKUS
Liar! He's dead. Nothing more than a rotting corpse in
Hades.

                    AMPHITRYON
Athena and Apollo raised him from the dead, blessed
through an enchanted grace to kill you.

                    LYKUS
I have a thousand mercenaries.

                    AMPHITRYON
All henchmen who will work for anyone meeting their
wages.
Oh sorrowful man, know you not how much joy Herakles will
have in his heart slicing and quartering all your men?
Surrender and live. Whatever you want is yours.

                    LYKUS
I shall never surrender to one naked beast! A man so old,
he can't even feel the stabbing pains of his rusted metal
on his backside. I'll have that flaccid penis of his cut
off as my gift offering to Hera.

                    (Exit LYKUS,
                    infuriated.)

                    AMPHITRYON
Such callous disregard to death's approach afflicts all
mortals. No one expects ill will to befall them. Rather,
everyone anticipates good tidings to warm their lives,

everyone born under lucky stars whose fates and destinies
will enrich them with wealth and power. Who ever thinks he
will encounter a consuming murderer in the tavern or draw
the attention of a stalking villain? All are innocent when
it concerns the expectations of a life well lived. Envy is
scoffed at, the warning set aside of a plot conceived
toward an ambush prepared to steal your soul for the glee
of a sadist.

No. Everyone thinks they are safe.
                    (Pauses. Sighs deeply.)
With a contented heart, with a conscience relieved, I
will tell Herakles of Lykus' decision. I swear, before I
die, I will witness Lykus' corpse falling in front of this
aged body. I will laugh a final time before I plunge my
spear through his skull. God, my laughter will roar without
hesitation when Herakles decimates the entirety of Lykus'
cohorts.

Who, more than Lykus, deserves to die for his innumerable
deeds of evil waged against all Thebans.

                                        (Exit.)

                                        (LIGHTS FADE.)

                                        (CURTAINS.)

                                        (END OF SCENE 1.)

ACT 3

Scene 2

SETTING: Inside LYKUS' palace.

AT RISE: Enter MEMBERS OF THE CHORUS,
                                      divided into twelve smaller
                                      groups. While each group takes
                                      its turn singing, the other
                                      groups continue dancing. As
                                      soon as one group completes its
                                      stanza, the following group
                                      instantly sings its stanza.

FIRST CHORUS GROUP

    Listen carefully. Roused Herakles crashes down the door
of Lykus' palace, his swift darting javelin thrusting
unmercifully hard into the assaulting mercenaries. Listen!
The hallways are filled with agonizing screams.
                    (The   audience   now   hears   the
                    frightening   shouts   and   pleads   for
                    mercy. The sounds of clashing swords
                    amplify.)
Requital for sin has stepped forward for payment. Listen to
Lykus' running feet, swiftly heading toward Hades' dank
cavern, the palm of his hand coinless for Charon's oars to
push his boat into Pluto's realm.

SECOND CHORUS GROUP

    Shout out your cheers! Justice prevails as Herakles
stands firmly at the doorway, his left hand thrusting his
javelin directly into the hearts of foolish and wayward
men, his right hand sword gashing open multiple chests, the
gapping wounds of his opposers spill their blood and
intestines to the floor where other rushing mercenaries
slip and fall toward Herakles' ankles. With a face firm in
its resolve, Herakles crushes their skulls. The river of
fate has abandoned the falsifiers, their frightening shouts
ebbing, echoing in miserable exclamation.

THIRD CHORUS GROUP

    Herakles do not waver or heed the refluent roar that
desires to adhere to your mind. Cast it aside! Let your
slamming spear offset the encroaching guilt. Through
grace's wondrous salvation from concealing Hades you rose

to perform death's penalty upon the souls of treacherous filth—

FOURTH CHORUS GROUP

. . . for their outrage against your wife and children, do not think of resting your arms or ceasing from your anointed task. You are the death-wielder who has been granted powers of victory by Zeus.

FIFTH CHORUS GROUP

Do not wipe your tears of regret. Transform them into tears of joyous reckoning.

SIXTH CHORUS GROUP

Now is the hour which Lykus never expected to come against him. His heart quivers with the realization that for all his cunning maneuvers, not once had he foreseen retribution's vengeance rising from the flames of righteousness!

> (All the MEMBERS OF THE CHORUS retreat to the backstage, gasping and covering their faces as six enemy soldiers crowd into the center of the stage with Herakles following them, slashing his swords against their shields and spears. The fighters briefly pause in the center stage, shouting and moaning, then resume their retreat to the other side of the stage.)

SEVENTH CHORUS GROUP

Friends of Thebes. Citizens! Praise Herakles' gallantry on your behalf. By the hundreds he vanquishes Lykus' soldiers. They retreat as he advances. What we have longed for is now our reality.

> (LYKUS rushed onto the stage, mingling within the MEMBERS OF THE CHORUS.)

LYKUS

Don't stop moving. I need a place to hide. Refuge and sanctuary for a lost man. A grieving man.
> (THE MEMBERS OF THE CHORUS push him toward the exit.)

Pitiful me! Grievous scorn dresses me as a saint dresses her hero. I am the hero, and this hero is lost to the vicious cruelty of a man gone insane with the lust of bloodshed. Anyone, help me.

> (Full exit.)

EIGHTH CHORUS GROUP
Rejoice! Lykus' cries are as sweet music to our ears! The chord of anticipation yearns to be sung. FREEDOM FOR THEBES! Let death's net remove Lykus and his cohorts far away from our walls.

NINTH CHORUS GROUP
Lykus shrieks with agony. Herakles' sword has found its final mark!

ALL CHORUS GROUPS COMBINES AS ONE
Our eyes moisten for we hear Lykus' prelude of slaughter! In cowardly anguish he screams!

> (LYKUS stumbles to the stage, holding his bloody sword.)

LYKUS
Who lives who can best Herakles' sword? Who lives who can dodge his spear or escape his javelin's thrust? His arrows fly true each time to fell his opposer.
In Kadmus' land, through treachery, I am murdered.
Hera, Lyssa, rescue me.

> (He holds his sword toward heaven before dying. The first six groups of the MEMBERS OF THE CHORUS lift up LYKUS' body, carrying it across the stage.)

TENTH CHORUS GROUP
The evil slayer who has murdered the innocent citizens of Thebes is himself slain.
> (HERAKLES walks onto the stage, crying. All other groups fall to the floor, also crying tears of anguish, except for the TENTH GROUP which walks steadfast among them, consoling them.)

Do not mourn for the betrayer and conniver of unjust policies, for he became the executioner of fallacious laws.
Vengeance, however, when it materializes, is always painful for the deliverer. Hush Herakles. Hush Thebans all. We have vanquished tyranny's wrath-filled days.

HERAKLES

A thousand men I slew this day. Though treacherous and abominable all, I cannot justify what I have committed against those lessor souls.

> (HERAKLES is lifted up by the cheering CHORUS as they lead him to the exit.)

ELEVENTH CHORUS GROUP

What man or force of power can circumvent the god's design for humanity? The grandly designed lawlessness conceived by Hera, Iris, and Lyssa has failed miserably to overwhelm our righteous cause.
We are the sentient beings of integrity, the holders of graceful energies set aside to enter a supreme paradise. The man, or the power, that attempts to praise the empowered Olympians speak for naught, for in truth, only we humans have given them the ability to rule us. Beware Olympus, your day shall soon end in a climatic rebellion.

TWELFTH CHORUS GROUP

Our enemies no longer live. A righteous execution the haters of justice deserved.
The palace has quieted. The servants wash the blood stains from the floor, preparing it for a festive celebration.
Prosperity shall once again adorn the streets of Thebes.

> (Exit ALL.)
>
> (LIGHTS FADE.)
>
> (CURTAINS.)
>
> (END OF SCENE 2.)

ACT 3

Scene 3

SETTING: Inside LYKUS' palace.

AT RISE: Enter MEMBERS OF THE CHORUS
                                     COMBINED AS ONE dancing
                                     joyously throughout the
                                     stage.

LEADER OF THE THEBAN ELDERS
Let us transform ourselves from mourners to dancers. Dry
all tears. Tear off your black cloths. Feast gloriously
this day our deliverance from hatred's greed.
    Divine Thebes! Open your shops. Bake bread, freely pour
wine. Herakles has saved us from our afflictions. The
chains of slavery have been severed. Sing, Thebans! Sing!
    "The tyrant is slain!" Broadcast it throughout Hellas so
all who dream of harming us will take cautious reflection
of who we are and who our heroes are!
    "The tyrant is slain!" Run to the port of Acheron and
offer sacrifices to Zeus. The wood is already chopped. Let
us henceforth sear unrighteousness away from our shores.
    "The tyrant is slain!" Let us trust the gods to provide
good tidings to us. May fortune, gold, and wealth return to
our city. May our merchants thrive and our explorers voyage
successfully to new harbors, boasting proudly to all: "We
are Thebans. No dictator rules over us. Power and glory to
the victor!"
    Ismenus, walk about, crowned with garlands.
    Invite your daughter, Dirce, to feast with us.
    Dance the dance of joy. Dance the dance of freedom!
Dance!
    Swim in the gentle currents of our waters, protected by
the daughters of Asopus.
    Nymphs, sing glorious songs to our hero, Herakles!
    Pythia, daughter of the Oracle of Delphi, Muses of
Helicon, join our celebration by praising throughout the
hallowed halls of Olympus Herakles victory over dreaded
scorn.
    Olympian gods of fertility, bless our women to birth
thousands of sons to replace the sons we lost to Lykus'
treachery. They shall become a sacred light to their
parents.

Newly weds, rush to bed. Copulate and bring forth boys to enrich our army. Teach them the laws of Theban civility. Honor your mothers and fathers. Honor Thebes and its altar. Honor Hellas.

Thebans, teach your children the tales of Herakles: how he ventured forth from inescapable Hades, renting in half Pluto's chains, then appearing mysteriously in front of the altar of Zeus to save us from tyranny's grip.

Herakles' birth is more than a divine miracle: it is a testament of self-sacrifice forever pledged to serve his friends, family, and country. Herakles is revealed glory!

The cause of righteousness has triumphed over evil. Lykus, the image of a vomit-covered man, is dead!

May the heavens receive his body, as worthless as it is.

> (Enter IRIS and
> LYSSA from above
> the stage.)

IRIS

Theban Leader, what happened to your good cheer, silencing so rapidly? Is it because you never expected to see the daughter of Night: Lyssa, or, her best friend: Iris, Queen of the Rainbow?

LEADER OF THE THEBAN ELDERS

What message does Iris bring us? Is it from Hades?

IRIS

Pluto brings all of his personal greetings. He happily waits for all of you to help him fill his multi-tiered mansion.

> (CHORUS MEMBERS hold their hands
> over their faces, running
> chaotically about the stage.)

Stop fleeing! There's no escape. We are not here to curse Thebes or shatter its seven-gates. We are not here to enslave anyone or carry away your children or beautiful daughters and handsome sons.

We are here for only one reason: to punish he who had murdered our servant and friend, Lykus.

LEADER OF THE THEBAN ELDERS

What one man could have murdered Lykus who had the protection of one thousand mercenaries?

                              IRIS
You stupid fool! Trifle not in these affairs.

                    LEADER OF THE THEBAN ELDERS
Why are you plaguing us.

                              IRIS
    Theban Elder, it is warrantless to be afraid of us. We
shall always do whatever we want regardless of all your
screaming and pleading. Herakles engaged in an unsanctioned
killing: his thirteenth labor rendered without Zeus'
approval.

                    LEADER OF THE THEBAN ELDERS
    Herakles has already completed his twelve labors without
fanfare or gratitude. Can he not for the fanfare and
gratitude of an entire city, not protect it from a tyrant
raging with an insane attitude toward all his subjects?

                              IRIS
    One thousand men Herakles sent to Hades, filling Charon's
boat time after time, his hands calloused, his arms worn,
his legs bruised. One thousand rooms Pluto had to prepare
to receive them. Among all his paid soldiers, where is
Lykus? Lykus held no coin in his hand to pay Charon. Now,
he wanders aimlessly, voiceless, purposelessly throughout
the frigid cold of the vast cosmos. His suffering is worse
than death because his soul extinguished before it could
adhere to a safe refuge.
    Yet, still live Herakles' sons and wife, Megara. Herakles
interfered with Pluto's timelines for their welcoming into
his mansion. Four rooms remain vacant. Four rooms need to
be filled. As Lykus was touched by an insane urgency to
enslave the people of Thebes, so shall a similar curse
befall Herakles who will fill Pluto's vacant rooms. Through
this, Herakles will finally yield to Hera's proper status
among the Olympian gods. Her husband/brother, Zeus, will
not protect his son for his vile attempt to cheat fate and
destiny of their set timeframes which have been allocated
to each person upon the moment of their birth. This is
Uranus' unbreakable law: no one may extend his life beyond
its measured frame.
    Therefore, our mission is to inflict upon Herakles an
insatiable appetite to slay his three sons during an
enactment filled with the suffering of an insane frenzy.
After his sons and wife have crossed the Acheron through

his own rage-filled hostility, then he will understand the depths of my hatred enacted against him.

LYSSA

From my parents came forth I: born from mother Gaea, the goddess of earth. Born from father Aether, god of light. Empowered with the talents of Nyx, I reside in Erebus where I was charged by Hera to protect her highly loved pet, Cerberus.

For my failure to protect Cerberus, for my failure to entrap Herakles, for my failure to enslave Theseus, for my failure to save Lykus from Herakles' destructive assault, and, for forfeiting Lyssa's soul, I have mandated myself to perform a reckoning of equality. The hero who has tamed the raging sea, civilized the country inhabited by fanatics, who fought against the mighty Amazons and won, these deeds have already brought to him extraordinary fame.

Now, in vengeance decreed, I will ruin Herakles' brilliant fame with one single, swift act. No longer will anyone remember his conquests and his triumphs. No one will stare at the constellations looking for his signs. Henceforth, he will be thought of as the "child-slayer" and "woman-destroyer."

IRIS

Lyssa, I will transform myself to look like Herakles' wife, Megara, encouraging him to drink all the flasks placed in front of him. Within a few moments, I will bring him to you so you may bestow upon his mind intensely filled memories of all his campaigns . . . terrifyingly so.

LYSSA

Do so at once. With hatred supreme, with firm determination, I will not set myself aside from this course. If Zeus hates me for it and condemns me, so let it happen. If I need become the whore of Zeus, imprisoned and taunted, so let it happen. Uranus shall be my defense that I am compelled to hurt Herakles to set straight the errors of him cheating Pluto from filling his rooms at designated time. No power can change the hour of death.
(In a deranged voice.)
Listen. I hear the sea-waves protesting my course of action. I see the bodies of dead sailors rising, desiring to attack me, for all want Herakles to live an unharmed life. How can this be, this murderer of men to be so fondly loved by murdered men?

Listen. Hear the thundering claps of thunder that strike all around me demanding me to avert, for Pluto has struck a wager with Uranus, the law modified so Herakles may live. I care not about their agreement. No judiciary will pronounce me guilty. Come earthquakes and try to remove me from my perch of obstinate desire to render Herakles insane and turn his famed heroics into deeds of squalor.

My fury cannot be abated nor turned away from. My destiny is set to destroy this mythological man into a quiet nonsensical whisper.

Come Iris, bring to me my target so I may rush upon his breast with fanged teeth injecting my uncurable poison into his flesh. I will fill his veins with the bloodlust of wolves and with the carnage of hyenas.

Yet, I will not slay him on my first attack. He shall wake and see his crimes, and in despair, murder himself. How then can Zeus or Hera hold me accountable? Pluto will praise me and, Charon shall eternally adore me.
> (She hears a rough, stumbling sound
> coming toward her accompanied by
> laughter.)

Look! I see him! He runs to me uncaringly. His gorgon-glaring eyes, filled with wine, places him directly in my path.

Look! The drunkard bellows like a sickened bull. His fiery panting betrays his aged body's inability to flee further away.

Howl, Herakles. Howl. Your dance is as clumsy as you are, flaying arms and tripping over your own feet. A jokester you are. A pathetic disease that ravages luckily wherever you strike: not through intellectual analyses or through the study of tactical maneuvers, but through the sheer folly of brute strength coupled with the luck of marksmanship.

Now, Iris, now, bring him closer to me. After I pierce his arm, fly to Olympus and brag to the world that I, Lyssa, alone overwhelmed mighty Herakles.

> (IRIS ascends.)

HERAKLES

Where goes Megara? Have I lost my wife in this darkened passageway?
> (As HERAKLES looks up, LYSSA swoops
> upon him, kicking him flat on his
> back. Instantly, her fanged teeth
> sink into Herakles arm, causing him

                to scream unbearably in agony. He
                tosses as he holds his arm up.)
My arm burns! It burns! What have you done to me, bitch!

LYSSA

Bitch? You called me that before inside the caverns of
Hades when you took from me Hera's beloved doggie.

HERAKLES

Lyssa? Why?

LYSSA

Because I absolutely detest every fiber of your being.

HERAKLES

It's not my time to die!

LYSSA

Everyone says that. So live. But, live forever confused,
your mind constantly filled with the inescapable horrors of
all your battles combined as one. Forever rage, for
everyone is your enemy, and, none more so than Megara and
your three sons. Quick, defend yourself. Your enemies
approach.

(Exit LYSSA.)

(HERAKLES begins screaming, shaking
and turning around on the stage
floor, kicking and thrashing about.
He stands up, collapsing again, his
arms reaching through the air, his
hands tightening, finding nothing.)

HERAKLES

Megara! Therimachus! Deicoon! Creontiades! Death and
dishonor to all of you. RUN! RUN!

(HERAKLES staggers off the stage.)

(LIGHTS FADE.)

(CURTAINS.)

(END OF SCENE 3.)

ACT 3

Scene 4

SETTING: Inside HERACLE'S house.

AT RISE: Enter HERAKLES and SERVANT.

                        SERVANT
     Master! Your arm! Why is it so terribly swollen?

                        HERAKLES
                     (In a trance.)
     My arm? I have no idea. Perhaps a dog bit me.

                        SERVANT
     Those are not the marks of a dog bite, nor a snake. It is
the mark of a sinister demon. Quick, allow me to treat it
before it festers and destroys your mind.

                        HERAKLES
     What? What?

                        SERVANT
     Let me help you.

                        HERAKLES
     Help me?
                     (Suddenly shouting.)
     Help a warrior who has triumphantly marched against the
most fearsome monsters conceived in hellish fashion. Help a
warrior who traveled from Hellas to Libya to Spain to
Persia, and to the northern frigid land of the Amazons.
                     (Pushes SERVANT away.)
     I am Herakles, untamed. Undefeated! What do you know of
pain and suffering? Of famine and thirst? What do you know
of youthful friends dying in your arms, their tears
unanswerable? I am Herakles, and for every man I destroyed,
for every monster I defeated, ten lifetimes of my life were
taken away from me. Oh, how can you know the terrible
anguish of lives lost? How!

                        (HERAKLES stands up as a group of
                        dancing actors dressed in ghostly
                        costumes rush upon the stage
                        followed by a second group of actors

> costumed as the a Lion, the Hydra,
> and Cerberus the dog. The entire
> group surrounds him, then opens up
> so the audience can see HERAKLES
> striking haphazardly at them.)

Come on! Come on! Fight! Fight!
Theseus - behind you.
Iolaus, run!
A sword! I need a sword. Come on! Fight!

> (HERAKLES runs among the reenactors
> of past battles, wildly swinging his
> arm as if holding a sword.)

Ahhhhhh! Ahhhhh! Ahhhhh!

> (HERAKLES falls to his knees,
> bawling.)

I can't save you. I can't save you!

> (He pushes away the entire group of
> assaulters and runs to the front
> center of the stage.)

I am discovered. I am the jokester of all follies!
Ahhhhhh! Ahhhhh! Ahhhhh!
My spear for a seer's heart! My bow and arrows for a
priest's heart!
Ahhhhhh! Ahhhhh! Ahhhhh! I can't save you!

> (Enter IRIS and
> LYSSA.)

LYSSA
Herakles. It is I, your betrayal, your abuser, your
mocker, Eurystheus.

> (IRIS rushes to LYSSA and places
> over her shoulders a male's robe and
> straps over her chin a man's beard.)

HERAKLES
No more labors! I am finished with them.

> (He charges against the disguised
> figure, grabbing hold of her neck.)

> > (Enter MEGARA, her
> > three sons, and
> > AMPHITRYON as IRIS
> > and LYSSA retreat
> > to the back of the
> > stage, remaining as
> > observers.)

> (MEGARA is holding in her hands a
> wine cup.)

MEGARA
Why are you shouting so? Why are so strangely fussing about.

HERAKLES
Woman! Can you not see I am saving us from Eurystheus.

MEGARA
Eurystheus is not here?

HERAKLES
His neck is in my hands.

MEGARA
You hold no one. Settle down. Drink.

> (When she tries to hand him the cup,
> he slaps it out of her hands. As she
> backs away, LYSSA and IRIS approach
> her and place over MEGARA'S shoulder
> the male's robe and straps over her
> chin the male beard.)

Why are you mistreating me? I revere you.

HERAKLES
Eurystheus, you revere me? You the source of all my problems. The originator of all my sins.

                              MEGARA
     Why are you talking like this? Your eyes! Why do they so
roll with such fright? OHHHHH! Your mouth foams as though a
rabid dog.

                             HERAKLES
     Eurystheus, until now, I never realized how much I hate
you. There is only one way I can absolve myself of my sins
. . . I need to offer you to divine Zeus as my pentance.

                              MEGARA
     What is wrong with you. I am Megara, your wife. Will you
harm me in front of your children and father in your
drunkard stupor. Rest, calm yourself.
                         (HERAKLES keeps moving sinisterly
                         forward.)
          Servants, restrain him.

                             HERAKLES
     Come, Cyclops! Come, Hippolyte. Today I own the
craftsmen's bars and measuring rods. Today I will destroy
all of you, including this city and all its citizens! I
will singlehandedly wage war against the entire world until
I have slaughtered from its surface all mankind. Theseus,
where is my chariot? Bring to me Diomedes' horses!
With the blood of men I will purify myself before I step
upon the throne of Olympus, my rightful rule achieved.
     Iolaus, arm me with my olive-branched club. I declare war
on Mycenae!

                             SERVANT
                         (Uncertain if he
                         should laugh or be afraid.)
          Is our master jesting with us, or is he truly insane?

                             HERAKLES
                    (As if galloping his horses.)
     Look! Nisus stands before us. Tear down its walls! No
mercy!

                         (He mock fight invisible soldiers.
                         Stops, walks over to the wine table
                         and calmly drinks as he smiles
                         broadly.)

     Onward to Isthmus. I need their trees for our sailing
ships.

>   (Again he resumes fighting
>   invisible solders.)

Victory! Victory at all costs! Die for me!

>   (He falls to the ground, flaying his
>   arms and legs as if wrestling. He
>   starts striking toward the floor as
>   if he is fighting an enemy soldier.
>   He begins laughing.)

Hear me! I am unbeatable! Die for me!

>   (He suddenly stops and stares at
>   Megara. She bolts off to the other
>   side of the stage.)

Eurystheus There's no place for you to hide.

>   (AMPHITRYON steps between them,
>   grabbing his arm.)

                    AMPHITRYON
Son!
>   (He slaps him.)
Stop whatever it is that you're doing. All of us are
afraid.

                    HERAKLES
                    (Crying.)
Afraid? Yes! I'm afraid! I've been discovered. I need to
hide. To Crete. Yes, I must go to Crete.

                    AMPHITRYON
Son, I will take you there. For now, rest.

                    HERAKLES
I have fought in too many battles. Killed too many men.
The blood of the dead afflict me.

>   (MEGARA cautiously approaches him,
>   gently touching his swollen arm.)

                    MEGARA
Husband. Rest.

HERAKLES
Not as long as you, Eurystheus, lives.

AMPHITRYON
Step away from her.

(HERAKLES pushes AMPHITRYON aside.
Therimachus intervenes.)

THERIMACHUS
Father! You don't know what you're doing. You act worse
than the wild beasts.

HERAKLES
Child of Eurystheus, why do you call me father when I am
your uncle, and, being your uncle am guiltless of your
death.

(HERACLES pushes THERIMACHUS down.
A group of dancers unfold a red
cloth in front of THERIMACHUS,
blocking the audience's view as
LYSSA rushes forward from the back
stage and bends over, holding an
arrow in her hand.)

THERIMACHUS
(Screaming as the group waves the red cloth.)
Noooo! Please. Noooo!

(The group lifts away the red cloth,
revealing dead THERIMACHUS holding
an arrow with his hands upon his
chest.)

(HERAKLES removes all his clothes,
standing naked.)

HERAKLES
Foul and sinister child of Eurystheus, in purity I send
you to Hades. Charon awaits you.

(The group rushes with their red
cloth forming a wall in front of
DEICOON.)

                              LYSSA
There, warrior, another child of Eurystheus.

                             DEICOON
Grandfather! Mother!

                    (Both grab HERAKLES's shoulders. He
                    flings both aside. DEICOON wraps one
                    of his arms around HERAKLES' calf
                    while he lifts his other arm toward
                    his face.)

Loving father, don't murder me! I am your son, Deicoon! Oh,
please, wake from your murderous rage. I am not Eurystheus'
son!

                            HERAKLES
Boy. Let go of my leg. It is better for you to die with an
arrow in your heart than a club to your head. Stand back
and swiften your demise. Otherwise suffer needless torment.

                             DEICOON
I won't let go!

                    (The group rushes forward with the
                    red cloth to cover DEICOON and
                    HERAKLES at the moment he raises a
                    chair up in the air. The audience
                    hears it crashing on the floor.)

                              LYSSA
   Well done, master warrior. His head and all his bones are
crushed and shattered

                            HERAKLES
   Yes, Eurystheus' second monstrosity is gone. Yet, his
pleads momentarily caused me to hesitate.

                              LYSSA
   Then, no time to waste! The worse one yet remains. The
pretender who dreamed to unite Hellas and afterward the
world is surely the most dangerous enemy of all. Look how
he resists you standing beside Eurystheus. His time to
enter Pluto's mansion is long past its hour. Look. Is he
not too pompous a figure?

CREONTIADES

Father, why do you want to kill me? With affection, I have obeyed all your orders.

MEGARA

Kill him, kill me as well!

> (The group places the red cloth in front of the two, shaking it intensely. MEGARA falls over its edge, knocking it out of the group's hands, her amputated arm rolling away from her. The group proceeds to layer the red cloth over both bodies.)

HERAKLES
(To LYSSA.)

Finally, I have struck down Eurystheus and his children. All lie dead at my feet. Now I am revenged, my hatred quelled.

LYSSA

No. There is yet the final slaughter. Amphitryon.

> (An intense array of stage lights brightens the room. Thunder and lightning sound out.)

> (Enter PHALLAS, the god of war. She is elegantly dressed, her helmet covered in yellow plums. She is carrying a long spear. Instantly she picks up a statue of Zeus and hurls it directly into Herakles' chest, knocking him out.)

PHALLAS

Lyssa. Iris. Be gone!

(Exit LYSSA and
IRIS.)

PHALLAS [CON'T]
Antikyreus, administer your hellebore to Herakles.

(Enter Antikyreus
with his medical
pouch. He quickly
examines HERAKLES.)

ANTIKYREUS
Lyssa injected a powerful stream into his veins. But, I
shall save him. Yet, would it not be better for him to die,
considering the carnage and the victims?

PHALLAS
It was long past their time to reside in Pluto's mansion.
Now, the four vacant rooms are properly occupied. Fate has
been satisfied.

ANTIKYREUS
Though I can save his life, I cannot restore his mind.

PHALLAS
Do what you can. The rest lies in Apollo's hands.
(To AMPHITRYON.)
We need to tie his hands behind his back with fettered
chains. When he wakes, he will remember what he did.
Remembering, he may continue his wrath.

AMPHITRYON
Wretched deeds indeed, yet here sleeps a giant of
strength, cursed forevermore. A husband who has wantonly
murdered his wife and children have no place in society. He
will wander as a hideous outcast, shunned even by the worse
of murderers and rapists. I will plead to the leader of the
Theban Elders to forgive him.

PHALLAS
Remind him that Zeus has already forgiven Herakles. I,
the god of war, also forgive him for I understand the
hidden anxiety and fears that linger inside a warrior's
soul. Athena, though my enemy, remains his protector as she
also forgives him.
Through Lyssa's foul abuse and evil enchantment, Herakles
committed a crime not through his own making. His legends

as a hero will endure while this atrocity will fade into a
remote curiosity.

      (Lights dim.)

               (Exit PHALLAS and
               ANTIKYREUS.)

               (LIGHTS FADE.)

               (CURTAINS.)

               (END OF SCENE 4.)

ACT 3

Scene 5

SETTING: Inside HERACLE'S house.

AT RISE: Enter the LEADER OF THE
                                     THEBAN ELDERS and
                                     AMPHITRYON.)

LEADER OF THE THEBAN ELDERS
  Grave grievances afflict Thebes! Let all our citizens in
every street mourn in saddened anguish! Our esteemed guest,
our greatest savior, Zeus' son, victimized by treachery,
has committed the most hideous crime of all.
  Silence your flutes. Set aside cymbal and harp. Find in
our hearts solemn forgiveness for the man who suffered
gravely through thirteen labors for our behalf. Herakles is
our benefactor. He is not our enemy.
  I know how hard it is for you not to rise up against him,
to throw him out of Thebes. I know you want to pelt him
with stones and crush him with extreme hatred, for all
heroes, in spite of their great deeds, should one folly
afflict them, then they become scorned and held in
contemptible disgust. Should you try to destroy him, you
will fail. You will only add to his burdensome griefs even
more griefs. If he can kill one thousand highly trained
mercenaries in less than a day, how much harm can he
inflict upon a city filled with untrained citizens? Set
inside your heart resolve. Let your love no longer be
filled with compassion and remorse. Our hero has become our
terrorist.
  Heracles is lost, caught in a nightmare of unresolvable
monsters. The poisonous plague of Night's daughter, a
Gordon more vicious than all the Hydras of the world, stole
upon Herakles' most vulnerable self, injecting his veins
with a filthy poison inducing madness upon his soul.
  I warn Lyssa never again to molest Herakles, an alarm of
salvation shall be implored to Zeus. A mighty curse to the
palace's invader: Enkeladus will hurl from the depths of
Mount Etna ten-thousand lightning strikes at Lyssa.

AMPHITRYON
  Let the bloodshed be cleansed from the house.
Priests, enter and sing your chants to remove any
Reminders of Lyssa's curse.
Let peace return to Kadmean land.

Allow, through your prayers to Zeus, to help Herakles
Lie through his memories of what he had committed,
Pray for his anguish to be recessed in oblivion,
Its frightful enactment dispelled through
a peace-filled sleep.

LEADER OF THE THEBAN ELDERS
Please, accept my sincere tears of remorse for you and
for your grandchildren.

AMPHITRYON
My suffering is deeply personal. Please, refrain from
broadcasting your apologies so loudly all the city can hear
you. I beg you not to pound your fists into your chest,
wailing, nor to cry. If you must create excitement, please
step as far away as you can from my house, because your
dirge will certainly rouse him from his sleep. Antikyreus'
medicine, though it contains a powerful sedative, I'm
afraid it may not be powerful enough. Should he wake too
rapidly, should he break off his fettered chains, should he
wake filled with hostility against the world, who can
prevent him from burning Thebes to the ground?

LEADER OF THE THEBAN ELDERS
I best abide by your desire and leave.

AMPHITRYON
You waited too long. Look. He writhes and stirs. He
stands up, the chains breaking loose from his wrists as if
never there. Quick, we must run and hide underneath the
roof's rafters.

LEADER OF THE THEBAN ELDERS
How can a father be afraid of his own son? Your
imagination exaggerates the danger.

AMPHITRYON
Beware my son's wrath.
I'm not afraid of death nor of being killed. I confronted
Lykus' kindling wood and I marched, barely armed, into
Lykus' dreaded center of his mercenaries' hall. No, I'm
afraid that should he kill me, my death would rouse in the
very heart of his mind an inextinguishable vice of dread
that can never be broken.
What greater risk is there than the anger of a man
obsessed with the memories of hell? If you need to pray,

then pray that Megara's relatives will not seek revenge against Herakles, for the war that ignites, will enflame all of Hellas.

CHORUS

How then I wish Hera had simply killed Herakles after he decimated Lykus' palace. The gods' plots require too great a tragedy for us to bear.

AMPHITRYON

I behoove all Thebans to run as far away while they still can, not stopping for a single moment until they reach the shores of Sparta or the colonies of the Euxine Sea. This city of Kadmus origin faces a terrible vindictiveness such as the world has never known.

(Exit ALL.)

(LIGHTS FADE.)

(CURTAINS.)

(END OF SCENE 5.)

ACT 3

Scene 6

SETTING: Inside HERACLE'S house.

AT RISE: Enter HERAKLES.

                    HERAKLES
                (Fully conscious.)
   How is it I'm still alive after getting bit in the arm by
a rabid dog? Incredible! How is it that I had never
realized how beautiful the earth is: filled with greenery,
deep blue skies, clear streams of water. And what a
magnificent rainbow! Translucent green, soft pink, wondrous
blue, enticing yellow.
   Yet, there is a vague memory lingering somewhere in my
mind that a terrible thing just happened to me? What,
though, I can't remember. Yet, there are unfocused images
swirling in front of me: brief interludes stirring now and
then of a man heavily breathing, his nostrils snorting
violently, his arms pained, his legs burdened.
   Why am I surrounded by the shafts of my arrows, bloodied?
Why is my shield turned upside down on the other side of
this room so as not to comfort and protect my sides?
   Wait. Why are my hands tied behind my back, fettered
chains entrapping me as though I were a boat anchored to
the dock so the mighty winds would not topple me over? What
is the meaning of these things?
   Have I re-entered Hades, or, had I never left and
everything experienced nothing more than a nightmare's ploy
brought about because of my consuming hatred of Eurystheus?
   No, I'm not in Hades. Sisyphus rock is nowhere near me.
Pluto's chants are silent. Ceres' sceptre unseen.
   Am I so distraught over a dog's bite that I have no idea
where I am?

                (Enter AMPHITRON carrying a tray of
                food.)

                    AMPHITRYON
   Son, finally you are awake. Look, I brought you your
favorite foods.

                (AMPHITRYON rushes to him, hugging
                him tightly. He begins crying.)

HERAKLES

Father, why are you weeping? There's no need to hide your eyes with your hands.
                    (AMPHITRYON   moves   away   from
                    HERAKLES.)
Father, why are you distancing yourself from your beloved son? Have I done something wrong against you?

AMPHITRYON

Yes, my son, yes. You have gravely hurt me.

HERAKLES

Is this why my hands are tied behind my back? What did I do to you?

AMPHITRYON

A grievous malady you enflamed against your father, against the Olympian gods. Even Zeus cried when he saw what you had done.

HERAKLES

Frightening words! Tell me everything.

AMPHITRYON

Is your mind straight? I mean, do you have any tendencies to lash out at anyone?

HERAKLES

Stop with this nonsense. Unchain me and tell me what I did.

AMPHITRYON

I will tell you the moment you promise me your mind is clear. I want assurances you will not suddenly rage into a hellish frenzy and kill me for speaking to you the truth.

HERAKLES

Why are you testing me thus?

AMPHITRYON
                    (Raising his eyes to heaven.)
Departed fathers, will you protect me if I unravel my son's chains?

HERAKLES

I will protect you. Tell me who tied me up like this.

                    (AMPHITRYON unbinds HERAKLES.)

                              AMPHITRYON
     Zeus bound you in these chains after he witnessed the
     extent of Hera's curse upon you.

                               HERAKLES
                              (Laughing.)
       Again Hera. I hope I wrecked grave acts upon her. Ruined
     her hair! Bit off another nipple?

                              AMPHITRYON
       Hush! Stop your maliciousness toward Hera. Leave her
     alone and perhaps she will leave you alone.

                               HERAKLES
       I, for this moment, will not antagonize Hera, my
     beautiful nemesis. Now, tell me honestly, what terrible
     thing did I perform?

                              AMPHITRYON
       Are you in such a stupor, so blind, so forgetful, you
     can't remember what you did? Or, are you deliberately
     pretending not to remember?

                               HERAKLES
       I only remember a large dog biting me in the arm. Nothing
     else.

                              AMPHITRYON
       All this time we're been talking, and not have you looked
     upon the shattered bones of Deicoon, or at the pool of
     blood underneath the arrow sticking out of Therimachus'
     chest, or Creontiades' and Megara's amputated body parts
     littering the floor? You don't see this horror in front of
     your eyes?

                               HERAKLES
       I only see a beautiful morning. A wondrous, enchanting
     thrill. Would you like to walk with me?

                    (AMPHITRYON   viciously   slaps
                    HERAKLES.)

                              AMPHITRYON
     Athena! Open his eyes! Make him see what he did!

                         HERAKLES
                  (Soft, detached voice.)
     Oh, what happened here?

                         AMPHITRYON
     You have waged an unnatural war against your own
     children.

                         HERAKLES
     War? I don't understand. Who has done these things to
     these innocent children?

                         AMPHITRYON
                  (Shouting, as he chocks his son.)
     You did it! You, your bow! Your swords! And whatever god
     you want to blame.

                         HERAKLES
     Why would I do such a thing? I don't believe you.

                         AMPHITRYON
                  (Falling down, bawling.)
     Because you're insane.

                         HERAKLES
     Is that a woman over there? I'm not sure, there are so
     many parts of her around.

                         AMPHITRYON
     She was your wife, Megara.

                         HERAKLES
     An inexplicable cloud shrouds me? Through it, I hear
     voices.

                         AMPHITRYON
     Voices? Lyssa's? Iris'? Hera's?

                                   (Enter LYSSA, IRIS,
                                   and HERA, bemused.)
                         HERA
     Not one tear shed.

                         LYSSA
     Not one thing remembered.

                              IRIS
Our long-worked-on plot means nothing. He'll leave
Thebes, go to another city, fall in love with another
woman. Marry. Have new children, fight a new battle, take
for himself concubines, and feast without a singe
reflection of what occurred during the night inside his
home.

                              HERA
Yes, all those things will happen. Athena and Zeus will
protect him fiercer than before, but before we leave,
Lyssa, restore his memory back to him before Zeus closes it
again.

                    (HERAKLES reels and falls down. He
                    crawls about the stage, realizing
                    what he did. He frantically screams
                    and cries.)

                            HERAKLES
Father! I murdered my own family. Blood's guilt adheres
to every pore of my body. GOD DAMN ME! GOD DAMN ME!

                    (He tries to bolt through the open
                    door. His father wraps his arms
                    around him.)

                          AMPHITRYON
Where are you going?

                            HERAKLES
Why haven't the Theban Elders arrested me? Executed me?

                          AMPHITRYON
What chains, what doors can hold you? All are afraid of
you.

                            HERAKLES
Then I must kill myself by jumping head first from the
nearest cliff.

                          AMPHITRYON
You'll survive the fall.

                            HERAKLES
Then I'll plunge the sharpened dagger into my heart.

AMPHITRYON
The dagger will break.

HERAKLES
The altar of Zeus has a vast quantity of kindling wood stacked beside it. I'll set all the wood on fire and jump into its center.

AMPHITRYON
Your jump will extinguish the fire and shatter all the wood over the cliff.

HERAKLES
Surely there must be a way for me to kill myself? Or, find someone who can kill me?

AMPHITRYON
None can kill you. You cannot even kill yourself.

HERAKLES
Hera can kill me.

AMPHITRYON
She tried since the day you were born, first placing two vipers in your bed, whose necks you broke, and throwing you into the volcano of Mount Etna which you flipped over.

HERAKLES
Am I then cursed to live for the rest of my life in shame and disgust? There's no place I can hide. Not even in Crete nor in Hades. Zeus! Please, cover my head in darkness. I am evil beyond evil. My blood is a contaminate filth. Rid me of it.
(Pauses.)
Silence is all I hear. My petition goes unanswered. Send Theseus to me. He'll know what to do.

(Exit.)

(LIGHTS FADE.)

(CURTAINS.)

(END OF SCENE 6.)

ACT 3

Scene 7

SETTING: Inside HERACLE'S house.

AT RISE: Enter THESEUS with ATTENDANTS
                                     and AMPHITRYON.

                          THESEUS
   Amphitryon, I hastened my horses the moment I received
your message. I left behind thousands of Athens' finest
warriors to recuperate their horses and sharpen their
swords near the clear-running streams of Asopus.
   Give this golden hammered spear to Herakles as a symbol
of Athens' friendship to Thebes.

                        AMPHITRYON
With all appreciation we welcome you.

                          THESEUS
   I read reports from the citizens of Erechtheïds
that Lykus has overwhelmed and murdered Kreon. This land's
sceptre shall be returned to the Thebans for we cannot
abide a usurper. Because war had come upon you, we shall
fight beside Herakles without hesitation or retreat.

                        AMPHITRYON
   The reports you have are old. Things have drastically
changed. The tide of discord, always wavering, has shifted.

                          THESEUS
   I noticed Herakles is not here to greet me. I hope
nothing has happened to him. Without his tactical skills
and unrivaled strength, I would still be trapped in Hades.
For his bold rescue, I am here, ancient one, as a firm and
true ally. My hand on this pledge.

                        AMPHITRYON
   Theseus, have you seen our streets?

                          THESEUS
   I made entry through the underground passages. I have
never known them to harbor such a thick reeking of filth
and decay.

AMPHITRYON
Come, let me open the curtains for you.

THESEUS
(Gagging and coughing.)
The streets are filled with decaying corpses! Look how stiff and swollen they are. I should never have lingered on the road, but I delayed in the hopes of recruiting more men to fight on Herakles' behalf. Due to my delay, many young men and women had been slaughtered. Had I hurried, regardless of the number of men under my command, I may have been able to save them.

AMPHITRYON
No, you would not have been able to save a single one of them. Lyssa the goddess taught me a very valuable lesson: death waits for no one. Cheat death, and its roar against you increases a thousand-fold.
If you don't believe me, just open that door.

(THESEUS walks to the right side of
the stage and opens the door,
swiftly slamming it shut.)

THESEUS
Those are not the bodies of men who fell in battle. They are the corpses of young children hacked and quartered. I even recognized the resemblance of female parts, though they are decayed and maggot infested.

AMPHITRYON
The children you saw, belong to Heracles. The woman was his wife.

THESEUS
The boys appear too young to have been indoctrinated into the passage of a soldier's life. Were things so critical under Lykus, all Thebans waged war against him? Where was Herakles in all this? Such outrage blinds the mind!

AMPHITRYON
My fifty-year-old son aimlessly wanders around the olive grove singing hymns to the trees, collecting flowers, fishing as he gazes at the clouds trying to image them as living beings.

                         THESEUS
     What happened to him? Did it have something to do with
Hades?

                        AMPHITRYON
     It had something to do with everything he underwent.
Finally, the labors became too much for him. Insanity
surges throughout his mind, exposing his thoughts to the
things harsh and detrimental. It's as he had touched one of
his own arrow heads which he had dipped inside the Hydra's
head. Being Herakles, the poison didn't kill him. It merely
emptied his mind.

                         THESEUS
     Is the answer that simple?

                        AMPHITRYON
     It's better than the one he gives me: I was bitten by a
dog in the arm. If his head wasn't so strong, I would hit
him with his own club, but it'll just splinter.

                         THESEUS
     A dog bit him? In the caverns he fought courageously
against the gods themselves. No, it wasn't Cerberus who bit
him. It was Lyssa injecting her poisonous vile into his
veins. Hera must have plotted the entire drama.

                        AMPHITRYON
     My son, who valiantly slayed the giants of Parthenope,
who lived alongside the volcanic fields of Cumae, couldn't
even slay a common fish today. What he catches, he carries
home, leaving it to suffocate on top of the table. Look,
he's home now, sleeping under the table.

                         THESEUS
     He sleeps with a veil over his eyes. Why, when it's so
dark in here.

                        AMPHITRYON
     To hide his shame from the world, he will not permit any
one's eye to look into his eyes. The smallest glance
frightens him, forcing him to shiver uncontrollably.

                         THESEUS
     Unveil his face. I rode long and hard to see my friend's
eyes.

AMPHITRYON

Son, please, remove your mantle off your face. Look, a beautiful afternoon sun colors the fields magnificently. It's a sight you shouldn't miss.
                    (HERAKLES refuses to move. His hands
                    shake. To THESEUS.)
Look at how much he suffers from his monumental burdens. Grief has never known such sorrow.
                    (To HERAKLES.)
Son, I beg you, look upon this aged fool who has lived far too long. Touch my beard, my knee, and tell me you'll endure against the hateful things you committed.
                    (Begins crying.)
Son, I don't know what to do for you.
                    (Pauses.)
Thebes is here. Greet him gently as he gently came to visit you. Do not rouse your anger, desiring more bloodshed. All weapons have been destroyed from this house.

THESEUS

Herakles. It's true. I am here. I had looked grandly to embrace a friend who saved me, but now, I sit beside you in misery. The darkness you are suffering through must be a terrible darkness for you not to speak to me. If you want, curse me and place all the grievances of your life upon my shoulders. I will bear your hatred with fond love. Slap me. Beat me, but don't idly sit here and do nothing. It is contemptible behavior!
                    (Touches his hand.)
Please, stand up and allow your truest friend to see once again your face. Stand up, not for my sake, but to defy the gods who revel in your surrender to life's gracious embrace.

(THESEUS removes HERAKLES' veil.)

HERAKLES

Theseus, have you seen what I did to my own children?

THESEUS

Yes. I saw. Never have I seen such an appalling violence. I would never have believed a father could perform such malicious hatred toward his own family.

HERAKLES

Did you unveil my face to tell me directly my sins, thinking I knew them not?

                         THESEUS
     You are not a god. You are flesh and blood, limited to
bear the things you can carry.

                         HERAKLES
     Zeus promised to create a constellation honoring me.

                         THESEUS
     Such an act will dishonor the starry glow of all other
stars.

                         HERAKLES
     You dare say such a thing to me? Run then from this land
so you may never have to look at the stars hoovering over
Thebes.

                         THESEUS
     Your threats do not frighten me as I know you love me too
much to harm me.

                         HERAKLES
     Love?

                         THESEUS
     Only love could have triumphanted over three treacherous
gods.

                         HERAKLES
     In the vices of near defeat something compelled me to
fight onward. I know not if it was for love or for honor's
sake, but I could not leave you chained to the walls of
Hades when it was I who asked you to help me in the first
place. I suppose I saved you, not for love's sake. Rather,
for pity's sake.

                         THESEUS
     For me, I will always attribute it to love.

                         HERAKLES
     A lover of friends and family would find it impossible
to murder his friends and family. But, that's exactly what
I did.

                         THESEUS
     Then let me weep for your soul so Zeus may find
compassion in his heart to restore to you your former
personality. This change affects me too gravely.

                              HERAKLES
     I hate Zeus. He forces me to fight when I don't want to
fight. He forces upon me terrible conflicts. Now, those
conflicts have destroyed my mind. Do you think that was his
intention? To transform me from one semblance into another.

                              THESEUS
     You have fought unparalleled battles from one end of
earth to the other end of earth. Who has traveled as far
and as wide as you? Who has faced such insurmountable odds?

                              HERAKLES
     Having undergone such trials, I am prepared to die, but I
find it ironic that I cannot die. Had I known that
beforehand, I would never have been afraid of the
calamities I had faced. Then, after fighting three gods
combined, defeating them, I believe I am capable of warring
against the entirety of Olympus. I believe the gods are
afraid of me. My children, my wife told me, were set to
become great kings. Hellas united under their rule, and
from them, descendants to rule the world. From my children
to their children, the whole world would be known as the
Grecian Empire - the earth renamed "Herakles".

                              THESEUS
     You boast mightily of future things that are impossible
to envision. More, you threaten to kill the gods. A mortal
challenging the immortals. As strong as you are, you are
not that strong.

                              HERAKLES
     You think my threats reckless?

                              THESEUS
     I think they are dangerous thoughts. If it were me, I
would never speak as you have spoken. Your words will
certainly destroy you.

                              HERAKLES
     That's what I want. To be destroyed. And, only the gods
can destroy me. So, why not die fighting the greatest enemy
of mankind: the false gods who please themselves making our
lives their callous entertainment.

                              THESEUS
     Hellas, nor I, want to watch you die such a frivolous
death.

HERAKLES

All deaths are frivolous. A soldier who rushes against
his enemy, hacking them until he conquers the barriers set
in front of him, is declared a hero with the wreath of
victory placed upon his head, but is he really a hero? To
save ten, a soldier kills eleven. The lines remain
balanced. But if a soldier refuses to kill one, resulting
in his line's destruction, he is called a coward, but is a
soldier of conscience, who refuses to kill, truly a coward?
I wonder if there exists a god somewhere who loves the
coward and hates the hero? In that god's eyes the soldier
who refused to kill enters heaven and the soldier who
killed is sent to hell.

I have killed monsters and warriors, all for naught.

Today I am a dejected coward. No god adores me. Not even
the beggar in the streets. I have lost the affection of all
Thebans, not one allowing me inside their house.

Theban law demands for me to vacate the city, to wander
aimlessly wearing upon my head the cloth of shame.

Now I must find a poet who will enhance my story, as seen
through my eyes, before the historian records the accuracy
of my vile self.

Theseus, I have no home. I am an outcast. Only Zeus' wife
is happy at my plight. Hera dances upon a marble floor
celebrating my disgrace.

THESEUS

Let her dance. While she feasts with her evil sharers, we
will leave Thebes and settle in the city of Pallas who has
already pledged his protection to you.

After you make amends with Athena, you will live with me
and share with me the treasures I earned after killing the
snow-white Minotaur of Crete who was given for its meal
fourteen Athenian children. Through courage, through
relentless devotion to the Athenian children you save
fourteen lives. Surely this vast number supersedes four
lives lost: lives already marked for Pluto's mansion.

HERAKLES

That fact does not comfort me.

THESEUS

Then think of this: your name shall endure its fame
throughout Athens. Marble statues depicting your victories
will be placed throughout the city, Athenians honoring you
in glory and admiration. Not one Athenian will talk of what
you did in Thebes. Not one poet, not one playwright. In

Athens, wherever you walk, Athenians will bow down and open their food and clothing stalls for you to take freely anything you desire.

                         HERAKLES
   Athens will do this for me? Ten-thousand thanks are not enough to express my gratitude to you for helping me during my direst need. Forgive me my tears that I cannot refrain from falling upon my redden cheeks.
                   (To AMPHITRYRON.)
   For my sake, for the sake of our love, for the sake of you being my father, please bury my children and wife with dignified prestige. For me, cry the dirge over their graves.
   After you completed your promise to me, remain in Thebes so the people will know that I did not fully abandon them. Should they need me, I will come to their rescue.
                   (To THESEUS.)
   From you I ask only one favor: that you permit me to have as my companion the ugliest feral dog in Hellas. With shorn hair I will walk throughout the city, content living in the forest, content in fishing, content in reflecting on the wonders of the sky. Should you see me eating from the lotus flowers, please do not stop me.

                         THESEUS
   Then let us leave, leaving sorrow behind. Enough tears have been shed. Place your arm around my neck and I will help you walk to your new city.

                         HERAKLES
   Here is my arm. Let it become a yoke of love. Before we depart, first let me embrace the man who raised me, staying with me throughout my trials, a truer father does not live than my father.
   Father, kiss me farewell for I have the greatest fortune possible for a man to have: a friend true in need.

                        AMPHITRYON
   Journey then beside a courageous friend renowned for his honesty and unwavering steadfastness.

                         HERAKLES
   Farewell, dearest father.

                        AMPHITRYON
   Farewell, dearest son.

HERAKLES

When you bury my sons and wife, I shall be with you,
secretly watching from atop the hill.

AMPHITRYON

I will gaze toward you and smile. Yet, who will bury me
when Pluto calls out my name?

HERAKLES

I . . .

AMPHITRYON

Then travel in safety and in love. Just promise me, when
the servants of hell come for my soul, you will not fight
them away. No man has the right to delay his calling.

HERAKLES
(Crying.)
Father, your heart and image shall always remain with me.
My only regret is that I have wasted my life fighting
battles so far away from you. Now, my body is worn out, my
muscles afflicted with searing pain, and with bent head I
will follow Theseus, begging always for his mercy. Fame and
wealth have eluded me. I have no kingdom. No honor. But
your love, I know, belongs to me.

THESEUS

Herakles, discard your fear. Not one Theban shall
prosecute you nor discard your triumphants. No one will
turn your legends into something hateful. Your reputation
will never tarnish and, when the people speak of you, they
will affectionately remember you as the savior of Greece.
No man shall have greater honor than you, for you
Herakles, are Herakles.

(Enter LEADER OF
THE THEBAN ELDERS.)

LEADER OF THE THEBAN ELDERS
(Singing.)
Hear our tears of regret.
Our eyes are filled with anguish.
All must heed Pluto's calling for our souls.
Before we depart, we kiss fondly your good name,
For Thebes has lost her best friend.

HERAKLES

In gracious humility I accept your song of forgiveness.
Life goes on, even though we must bear in our hearts the
sins of our lives.

           (Exit.)

           (LIGHTS FADE.)

           (CURTAINS.)

           (END OF PLAY.)